DISTANT LIGHT

TALES FROM THE EDGE - BOOK 1

CHLOE ADLER

Signum Publishing

COPYRIGHT

DISTANT LIGHT BY CHLOE ADLER

Book 1 - Tales From the Edge

ISBN: 978-1-947156-35-7

© Cover Art: 2023 Rebeca Covers ©
Editor: Elizabeth Nover - Razor Sharp Editing
Proofreader: Deaton Author Services

ALSO BY CHLOE ADLER

Shadow Sisters

Mortal Desire, Dark Craving, Fevered Heart, Wicked Hunger

Tales From the Edge

Distant Light, Radiant Light, Blazing Light

Chronicles of Tara

Synergist, Planeswalker, Keystone

Destiny Chronicles

Descent, Dedicated, Devotion

Danger After Dark

Paris, Venice, Barcelona, London

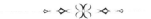

Dearest Reader,

This is book 1 in the series—Tales From the Edge and if you despise cliffhangers, you may want to chuck this in favor of a nice Italian soda or perhaps a hot chocolate. Though, and I may be biased, you will missing a fun roller coaster of adventure and love. Instead, why not read this book and move on to book 2! Problem solved!

This story follows Iphigenia Holt—the youngest of the witchy sisters (each sister has her own book in the series Shadow Sisters). The love scenes do scorch and are appropriate for ages 18 and above.

Join Chloe's Newsletter and grab a FREE Novella! Fire and Fangs is a sexy, enemies to lovers, multiple partner/why choose paranormal with sword-crossing. https://BookHip.com/QFGLCWZ

Circus Forever!

And now… onto the show!!!

XOOX ~ Chloe

"Shine so brightly that you illuminate a pathway for others to see their way out of the darkness."

~ Dr. Stacey A. Maxwell-Krockenberger

CHAPTER ONE

IPHIGENIA

I'm halfway through my morning yoga routine when my mother bursts into my room without knocking. I don't really mind her coming into my room uninvited—she's never done anything else—but she has a knack for doing it at the worst moments. How does a twenty-year-old woman living at home get her mother to take her seriously from Happy Baby pose?

By getting her butt off the floor, for starters.

I release my feet and bring my legs together before letting them drop to the floor, then use my abs to roll up to my feet. My lumpy bedhead bounces on my shoulders with the motion. "What do you need, Mom?"

"Iphigenia . . ." She reaches for a sweaty curl that's fallen in front of my eyes, trying to smooth it down behind my ear. Conveniently, she's too focused on it to look me in the eye.

My stomach drops. I know where this is going. Even without the waves of her guilt and worry swamping me.

"I know tomorrow is opening night and I know you want me to see you perform but," she bites her lip, "I just can't."

Of course she can't. Even though she doesn't tell me to stop performing, she hates what I do. And fears it. Never mind that it's the most important part of my life. I step back, then take a seat at my vanity, and pick up a hairbrush. "Mama, of course you don't have to go."

"I just can't watch you doing something so dangerous. It might give me a heart attack. Or I'd be the one in the audience yelling, 'Be careful, dearest, don't fall!' and what kind of show would that be?"

In front of the mirror, I yank the brush through my hair, flattening the frizz, and pulling everything into a smooth, tight topknot. "I understand, really. I've been performing for years, it's not like it's my first show or anything."

I start adding bobby pins to keep the shorter bits in line. My own mother has never set foot in the big top on the Edge's pier, never once seen any of the acts that I spend so many hours of my life perfecting, but I don't dare point that out. One of the pins snags, ripping out a few hairs by the root before I shove it back in.

At least she's being honest about her emotions for once. She really *is* terrified at the thought of watching me. Even now, her fear is palpable, like a thick, cloying blanket. Once the final pin is in place, I'll smother everything with hairspray. Once I'm done, I could do two sold-out shows back to back in June in a tent with no air conditioning and not have a hair out of place. Assuming it didn't give me a whopper of a headache first.

I must accept Aurelia for who she is, not who I wish her to be. "Besides, if you don't go, that's one more seat Serlon can sell." I summon a wink to let her know I'm kidding.

"I knew you'd understand, darling." Her face twists into a pained grimace. I think it's supposed to be a smile.

My mother, Aurelia, has never given up her formal upbringing and at 188, it's far too late for her to change now. "I thought you were staying in today to rest up for the show. Why are you *primping*?"

My arm falls from its position and my shoulders slump but I shake it off, prying open a bobby pin with my teeth. "I'm not primping. I'm figuring out how to style my hair for tomorrow."

"Do not use your teeth to open those pins, child. You could chip them. You don't want to walk around at 110 with missing, chipped teeth, now do you?" Her eyes watch me in the mirror, assessing. Her icy blue eye is cold and calculating. Instead, I focus on her brown eye, which I choose to see as warm and inviting.

"Yes, Mother, of course." Despite the curt words and penetrating stares, concern pours off her in waves. Sometimes being an empath sucks—often when I'm around my mother. Her emotions are intense and all-consuming, but she works so hard to hide them. With a normal person, I sense their feelings as they experience them, but when they're directed at me, I sense them ten-fold. And Mother puts up a good front, but underneath, she's never been one to curb her feelings.

Her mood is so intense today I actually pick up flashes of her thoughts. She's picturing me as a grown woman. She's given me a dewy complexion and flaxen corkscrew curls cascading down my back. Then I smile and all four of my top front teeth are chipped. Nice.

Sighing, I lean back in my chair, pausing in my preparations. Picking up my pale-pink, hand-blown water glass, I hold my mother's intense gaze in the mirror, take a sip, and then force a smile. "Of course, Mother. I won't use my teeth anymore."

She lets out a long, slow breath and offers me a curt nod but the image of me in her head now includes a full set of gleaming chompers. Crisis averted, I smile inwardly until— "Where did you get that glass?"

And just like that, Mother's calm is gone again. My gift—and sometimes curse—is to feel emotions, not predict them. Otherwise I would have prepared a diplomatic response. "Chrys made it for me." I take another sip before returning it to the glossy surface.

Concern oozes from her like endless scarves from a magic hat. "When. Did. She. Start. Blowing glass." Her teeth are clenched so tightly that my own jaw aches.

"She's taking a class at the art academy. Completely supervised. It's safe; she's not in any danger."

Aurelia's jaw softens, unclenching. "Not my concern. Your sister made her own choices to betray me, so why should I care about her?"

The question is rhetorical. Mother talks a good game but the pain she's hiding cuts deeply indeed.

"Anyway," she tosses her strawberry-blond waves over a shoulder, "I came in to tell you to stay in your room for the next two hours. The movers are

5

arriving momentarily with Alistair's furniture and I don't want you to get in the way."

That is not what she's picturing in her mind though. She's imagining me sauntering out into the hallway in my skintight work-out clothes and a group of men's jaws dropping to the floor like cartoon anvils. She even adds falling furniture to her imaginary scenario.

I cough to cover my giggle, pretending the hairspray went up my nose. If she knew I could see into her head, I don't know what she'd do. Aurelia is the most private woman I know. She's also the most dramatic.

I clap my hands together, distracting both of us. Sudden, unexpected sound does wonders to jolt people out of their thoughts. "That's right, today is the day. Are you ready?"

Mother's clipped features scrunch up as she snorts. She hides everything, even excitement. Will she ever tire of this game? Even Alistair can see through it, and vampires don't have an empathic bone in their bodies. I wish she didn't feel the need to hide so much of herself from the world. If only she let people see how amazing she was, everyone would love her as I do.

The doorbell rings and she scurries out of my room, calling, "Alistair, they're here!"

I remain sequestered, listening to the murmuring, deep voices of at least three different men. Soon the sounds of a dolly being rolled across the floor commence as I turn back to my not-primping. My older sisters primped, even Chrysothemis, and they ended up moving out and playing house with their boyfriends. Yet I belong here with my mother. No one understands her better than I do. My two sisters were unable to offer her unlimited help and the respect she requires. Everyone has their own path. Aurelia pretends to despise my sisters so I shower them all with unconditional love.

My updo figured out for tomorrow, I move onto the yoga mat. First my side splits and then my middle ones. I'll never be a full-fledged contortionist but with daily stretching, I am getting closer. Blocking out the thunk of boxes and the army of booted feet outside my door, I sink into my routine, happily shutting off the world and tuning into my body. After I finish my stretching, I review my choreography for the show until my body screams that it's time to expel the water I drank earlier.

Opening my door, I chance a peek around the corner. The coast is clear and my heart rate returns to normal. I do not want to run into my mother when she's in moving mode. Alistair's basically been living here since he and Mom became an item eight months ago, but moving him in is a much bigger deal. She still loves and misses my father, after all.

I step into the hallway and rush to the bathroom, eyes toward the living room to avoid the movers . . . which is why I smack straight into a very hard, very broad chest.

"Sorry!" I shriek without looking up. I try to sidestep into the washroom, but Broad Chest sidesteps in the same direction.

"Excuse me." Broad Chest's voice is so deep and warm it could melt a glacier.

I can't help but follow Broad Chest up to Solid Shoulders, then to Corded Neck, Kissable Mouth, and Eyes to Drown In. Bad follow-through. He's tall, muscular, tanned, and wearing no shirt. Great. I chalk the little surge in my heart up to adrenaline. Just the surprise of running into someone, literally. Must be that.

Without saying a word, I duck under his side, barreling into the bathroom, and slamming the door behind me. Once inside I pray to the Goddess that Mother did not hear the slam—it's something my middle sister, Sadie, did constantly throughout her teens.

I can almost hear my heart beating as I do my business and wash my hands, risking a peek in the mirror. My face gleams with a thin sheen of sweat. It is summer in Southern California, after all, and we don't have AC. I open the bathroom door after splashing cold water on my face. Surely the hunk—I mean, the gentleman is gone.

"I wanted to introduce myself."

One foot across the threshold, I squeal.

"Sorry," he steps back, "I didn't mean to startle you."

"What's going on?" Mother stands in her bedroom doorway, nostrils flaring.

"Oh, darling." Alistair's arm shoots out from behind her, circling her waist, and she visibly relaxes against him. He peeks over her shoulder and smiles. "Iphigenia, I see you've met my grandson Rhys."

"Grandson?" Carter has another brother? And Chrys never introduced us? I will be having *words* with my oldest sister . . . And impossibly, he's another stunning vampire. The clichéd apple sure didn't fall far from the tall, dark, and handsome tree.

Rhys extends his hand for the second time, a broad smile lighting up his dark-brown eyes, so deep and smoldering they remind me of a rich cup of espresso. His features are similar to those of Chrys's boyfriend, another one of Alistair's grandsons. But where Carter milks his bad-boy look, Rhys is more a dark Renaissance angel. His gentle curls lick his shoulders, and an aristocratic nose tops high cheek-bones and a kissable mouth.

"Iphigenia," Mother scolds. "Close your mouth before a bug flies in."

My face heats and I look away without shaking his hand. Far from offended, Rhys smiles wider, the stretch lighting up his face. His body blocks my escape to the hallway. Great. Tall, dark, and obviously no good is making fun of my discomfort now.

Rhys leans an arm against the wall beside me. "Grandfather tells me you're a circus performer."

"Yes—"

"That's enough." Mother's harsh voice rings out, and everyone's heads snap toward her.

"Darling," Alistair pulls my mother back into the bedroom, "there's no harm in the children getting to know one another."

Mother snorts. "Don't forget why you're here. We need you to *move furniture.*" I can sense her relenting though, and in a moment, she follows her man back into their bedroom.

As soon as they're out of earshot, Rhys whispers, "I'd really like to see you perform." The way he says it is matter-of-fact, without a hint of flirtation. How refreshing. And yet, a little pang trickles through me. Here's a complete stranger who wants to watch my act when my own mother refuses.

At least I'm more in my element talking about what I do. I smile up at him. "Tomorrow is opening night. If you'd like to come, I can get you free tickets."

"I'm a patron of the arts. I'm happy to purchase tickets and support the circus."

I twirl some fallen strands of hair between my fingers and am about to ask what he does for a living when Alistair's booming voice calls Rhys back to work.

Rhys

*T*urning away from Iphigenia is like turning away from the sun and ducking into a walk-in freezer on a frigid winter day in Alaska. I want to turn back and stare into those crystalline-blue eyes one more time. Eyes that promise sunshine on a rainy day, eyes that sparkle like rainbows, eyes that could bring a dead man back to life.

"Rhys, can you help me move this dresser?" Grandfather says even though he could easily carry it himself with one hand.

Vampiric strength has its advantages, no matter where I go. Until I've gotten enough capital to start my dojo, I can always get moving jobs. Here in the Edge, it's a little more difficult since the vampire population is abundant, but back in New York I always had a side gig to fall back on during slow seasons. Though I had to hide what I was there. Otherwise, I attracted the lookie-loos or the suckmouths.

"Why is the boy just standing there?" Aurelia says.

Ah, so that's why Grandpa is making work for me. Ah well, I guess I didn't move fast enough. "Caught in thought like most youngins." Alistair chuckles, putting a hand on her shoulder.

She sniffs. "I hope his thoughts aren't centered around my daughter."

"Ma'am, I'm here to help Grandpa and you." To underline the point, I pick up Grandpa's dresser and set it against the wall he indicates. "But to ignore your daughter's beauty and grace would be a disservice to you both."

Her eyes narrow.

"It's obvious where she gets it from." I flash her a smile and she blushes, picks up a box she just brought in here, and darts away.

A door down the hallway opens and I busy myself in the bedroom, straining to listen with my heightened vampiric senses.

"Iphigenia," says Aurelia.

"Yes, Mama?"

"If I were to lose you, I don't know what I'd do." Aurelia's voice is raised. She must know that both Alistair and I can hear her.

"You're not going to lose me."

"Rhys is not a stray. Do you hear me?" she hisses. "I know how much you like to collect them."

"I thought you loved Armageddon."

She sniffs. "That cat found *you*, like most animals. But Iphigenia, my home is not a zoo, and if you had your way. . ."

Iphi sighs, "Yes, Mother."

"Good. Then put Rhys on your list of strays-not to pick up."

"Mother!"

"Subject closed."

Wow, her mother is ripe. I have to choke back my reaction, which would be to defend her against this rampant shaming. What a lovely quality to possess, caring about animals and the less fortunate. Her mother makes it sound more like a curse. If Gramps didn't have to live with this woman I'd get in her face about the way she's treating her daughter, and to insist that I'm anything *but* a stray... anymore.

"How's your brother?" Grandpa asks. The ques-

13

tion throws me, and my mouth gapes while I think of an innocuous lie.

I haven't told him. I haven't told anyone, except my cousins. Though they're more like brothers to me than Nolan ever was. Plus they're cops, keen on helping our family and completely trustworthy. Straightening, I pretend to adjust the dresser. "Fine. We haven't talked in a while."

"What? Why? You two are practically conjoined twins."

I shrug, keeping my back to him. "You know, people grow apart. Interests change." I hate lying to him but the truth is so much worse.

I came to this town on a mission. But Iphigenia is much, much more than I expected. After meeting her, though . . . Well, hopefully she'll turn out to be only a small part of this mess.

CHAPTER TWO

IPHIGENIA

*E*arly the next evening I'm backstage getting ready for my performance. Since our circus is seasonal, I mostly teach during the off-season. But during the summer, I love to shine. And though I am proficient on several aerial apparatuses, my favorite is the silks. Out of all of the apparatuses, "silks" are the most ridiculously named. Two long pieces of material hang from a single point in the ceiling, but they're not made of silk. Fabric is the closest to what they really are, but of course that doesn't sound nearly as sexy.

"Iphi, up in ten," the house manager, Rodrigo, calls.

"Sure thing." I finish sticking on the last of the little purple jewels around my eyes with spirit gum.

Every year the circus has a different theme and

this year it's an underwater one. So I designed a mermaid costume. The base is a shimmering pink-and-blue bodysuit. I painted scales over tights in the same colors. Completing the outfit, my superhero-style cape glimmers with hues one shade darker than the bodysuit and tights. My hair is twisted up into a topknot, in which is nestled a bright-pink seashell. I've teased out a few curls to cascade down one side.

Peeking out at the audience from behind the curtain, I spot Rhys sitting in the front row. He's talking with someone to the right—a man with surfer-scruffy blond hair. In SoCal, he should blend into the background, but he has piercing blue eyes, arresting even from a dozen yards away. Just spying Rhys and his mystery companion there in the audience causes my hands to sweat and bile to tickle my mouth. Ew. On Rhys's other side are two more hotties talking to each other. Do good-looking men flock to Rhys, or did he stop at a beefcake modeling convention on his way here?

The music starts and I take the twenty seconds to check my hair in the mirror next to the curtain, reclipping a few sparkly pins. I pout at my reflection. Shoot, my lips aren't glittery enough. Should I run back to my dressing room to add more silver lipstick? No, no time.

Pulling in a deep breath of air, I smooth my

costume over my body, blink prettily at myself, and raise a shoulder like I'm posing for a photo. What the heck? I've never done that before. Geez, Iphi, pull it together, this is about skill and strength, not how pretty you look. With a huff, I spin away from the mirror, keeping my eyes trained ahead to avoid the pull of looking back at myself one more time. I've been the circus's opening act for years now. Where have these jitters come from?

On stage, Alexis, our ringmaster, is working the crowd. "Tonight you're in for a treat. Our amazing Iphigenia, the Flying Seraphim, will be performing a brand-new, never-before-seen silks act. Put your hands together and welcome our young phenom to the stage!"

It's true, I lied to Mother last night, but in my defense it was a white lie. I just didn't want to worry her. My palms are slick again, which is not what you want when you're about to climb twenty feet into the air. I dunk my hands in a bucket of rosin, suck in a large breath of air, and rub them furiously together before stepping into the spotlight.

I've been performing in the circus for so long that it's easy to filter out the applause. I paste a smile on my face and sweep my eyes over the audience, but I never really see them. I can never pick out any one person as my gaze blurs and roams. Their mouths move but I never really hear any sound. It's a routine, practically a meditation. With it, my brain disconnects as my body arrives on stage.

Yet my traitorous body strays from the routine tonight. My gaze unblurs and picks out Rhys in the front row. He's composed, a sly smile enhancing his stunning features.

Now that I'm close enough to sense them, his emotions are an almost tangible swirl. He's more excited than anything, a thrill he shares with the audience. But Rhys is worried, too. Strangers often hope they'll see a calamity—though most would have the good grace to be embarrassed if I called them on it—but Rhys is genuinely concerned for my safety. There's a warm thread of something else winding through his thoughts, too. He's picturing himself alone in the theater, watching me. Wait, no, not alone. The handsome man to the right of him is there, too. What on earth? But I have no time to dwell on that right now.

With an improvised flourish, I twirl and remove my cape, tiptoeing over to the expansive, flowing material. Serlon, the circus's owner, had this apparatus designed specifically for our underwater themed show. The blue-green material shimmers and sparkles under the hot lights. Hand over hand I climb, not using my legs at all until I'm partway up. I focus on relaxing my face into a smile, making it look easy. It's anything but. Gathering enough strength to do this particular move took me years of methodical, extensive training. My arm muscles tense and contract while the muscles on my back ripple, pulling in toward my spine. I used to find the shouting deafening, but now it blots out the world, smoothing out everything but my body and the feel of the silks around it.

Holding on to the fabric, I shoot my lower body into the air feet first and hook a knee over the top, above my hand. Two blissful moments of rest. Wrapping the fabric around my waist with one hand, I begin executing a series of moves, dropping a leg to throw the thick material over it and stopping to hold a pose. Aerial is a mix of strength and poise. An artist hits a pose to relax, but those are the moments when the audience cheers.

It's true that I've never done this exact routine in this exact order for an audience before, but most of these tricks I know by heart. I shift and soar between each pose, climbing and dropping, spinning, and freezing. Most performers, including myself, use an excruciatingly long drop for their finale.

So for my own, I fly up the silks to the apex of the tent. The pounding of my heart drowns out all other sound. I raise my head to the roof so no one will see me smacking my bone-dry lips.

Thump, thump, thump goes my heart.

I haven't done a starfish drop in more than a year. The last time I did one, a Tracker cut the silks and I plummeted to the floor thirty feet below. That moment of free fall lasted far too long as my both my heart and my body somersaulted over each other all the way down.

Here, now, jagged barbs of icy fear keep me poised above for a beat too long as my limbs chill and then go numb.

I spent the first six months after my fall avoiding the drop altogether, then the next six practicing it again and again. First from a short height, then incrementally higher—but never in a live performance.

Relax the face, relax the face, I chant in my head as I let go and tumble down. This time the fall takes on a personality. She is fickle and taunting, and I flail, pinwheeling in the air instead of the elegant descent with sleek lines I'd planned.

No, this won't do. I start at my face, relaxing my pinched expression, teasing out the furrows between my brows, reminding myself to breathe. *Check.* One hand crosses over the other as I find my rhythm. *Check.* Foot after foot I tumble, descending while the ground blurs. Arms and legs in line with the body, but not so rigid that I turn into a board. *Check.* Tuck the elbows and point the toes. *Check.*

Smile, Iphi. Keep breathing. Check.

My mind clings to the mechanics as the dread slips away.

After a few feet, it's seamless. The crowd is on its feet, though silence still reigns in my head. A few feet from the ground, I push myself straight out and unwrap my body. I've worked long and hard on this dismount. Holding tightly to the fabric with my hands, I push myself off with my feet, and I twist mid-air into a double flip before landing like an Olympic gold medalist, my hands raised high above my head.

The sounds of the audience bleed back in as I take my bow. Everyone is standing and screaming, but that group of men in the front row—Rhys and his companions—they're staring at me with more than simple appreciation. A flush that has nothing to do with physical exertion covers my face.

As I exit backstage, the other performers pat me on the back and congratulate me. I go back to rest in my dressing room before my final act. I'm the circus opener *and* closer. Give them something to make them stay and then give them something to make them come back. That's me.

The part I play in this circus is not lost on me. The circus pulls in its share of lecherous men and Serlon doesn't hide the fact that he uses whatever it takes to pack the seats. It's not why I chose to be in the circus, but it's a fact nonetheless. Until tonight, it was just a means to an end: skimpy outfits mean we don't all go home broke.

Tonight is different. Tonight I'm pleased to be wearing this skintight outfit that highlights all my curves. Though Rhys and his merry men would have been captivated regardless, the outfit mirrors my confidence. Respect for my craft poured off them. But that wasn't the only reason they couldn't look away. That I don't want them to, though, will make the closing act all the more interesting.

CHAPTER THREE

CASPIAN

Watching Iphigenia perform was intoxicating. She flitted up those silks like a butterfly. Effortlessly, weightlessly. My breath caught every time she dropped, especially at the end, when her face quite nearly met the floor. I jumped out of my seat and so did my brothers.

Rhys, who has been eying me throughout her performance, leans over. "I told you so."

Since we moved here, only Rhys has been on surveillance duty when she's practiced. It's the first time the rest of us have gotten a chance to see her perform, though I've seen plenty of her elsewhere. I can't help but wonder if Rhys is interested in Iphigenia for more than just her act—perhaps for something beyond "the job"? The way he's looking at me, it's like he's trying to plant a seed. We've shared women before, after all. The three of us would make quite the tableau together . . . though the picture in my head falls apart a breath later. Not every woman wants to be our centerpiece.

We make our way outside after the show amid the throngs of people exiting.

"You weren't lying," Thorn adds. "Do you think she could teach me some of those tricks?"

"Looking for another death-defying sport to add to your repertoire? She could try. That's her full-time job the rest of the year, teaching aerial. But," Rhys looks him up and down and snickers, "your body weight alone . . ."

Thorn gestures at his bulk. "What? So I'm not a Slim Jim like you. More weight to pull myself up with."

"Keep telling yourself that," I say.

"Is it always this crowded?" Dominic waves around the tent.

"I don't know. I've only seen the rehearsals. But it *is* opening night," Rhys says.

"Of course. And that girl is quite a draw. So, how should we approach this?"

"Meeting her?" asks Rhys.

Dominic nods.

"Less is probably more right now. After all, this is *her* night."

"Truth."

We file outside to more than one appreciative female giggle.

"One for each of us," a girl croons to her posse.

I don't blame them, and it wouldn't be the first time we've dated in a group. Women tend to notice us when we're all out together, and when they find out we're all brothers—well, we don't go home alone if we don't want to. It's fun for everyone—until they discover that we are actually a different species. Then eyebrows go up and uncomfortable questions get asked. Maybe that won't be as much of a problem in the Edge, the original Signum enclave.

Well, almost all brothers. According to the family tree, Rhys is just a cousin. But after spending so much time with us, he acts more like a Vidal than a Rees. Growing up, he even took our last name—because we teased him mercilessly for being Rhys Rees, or so I thought at the time. But now I suspect it was because he considered himself one of us. And he *is* one of us, one of my brothers. After all, his "real" brother left him. We didn't.

"Hey, man." Rhys clips me on the shoulder. "Can you quit eying the local talent? We're here for Iphi."

I snort. As if anyone else here holds a candle to Iphi's flame. Another example of the physical types misunderstanding us creative types. I'm about to school him when Iphi comes into view.

There she is. The girl is radiant, still in her sexy-as-hell outfit, except her cape covers some of the view. I can't say I'm not happy to see that, as the idea of random men leering at her does not sit well. She doesn't look like she just expended massive amounts of energy exhibiting inordinate strength. She looks refreshed and relaxed. Perhaps she's like Rhys and Thorn in that way. After Rhys teaches a class or after Thorn goes skydiving, they're both bouncing off the walls with energy for a while. It's like working out is food for their souls. Or maybe she's hopped up on adrenaline.

The moment our gazes lock, a surge of warmth floods my system. The sensation is almost overpowering. And we haven't even spoken . . . yet. I recognize the woman she's talking to from surveillance. Chrys is taller but alike enough that no one would miss the familial resemblance. She doesn't notice our exchange and keeps talking. All too soon, Iphi looks away and back at her eldest sister.

A low growl sounds to my left. I throw out my arm to stop Thorn from leaping forward. After a moment, he settles. The four of us talk amongst ourselves, mindful of Iphi's privacy.

"Does she know?" asks Dominic.

"I don't think so." Like all of us, Rhys is engaged in the conversation, but his gaze keeps straying toward Iphi.

"How can that little slip of a girl have so much power?" growls Thorn. "And why is she so damn sexy?"

"Hey, guys," I throw my arms up, "let's not objectify her." *Aloud, anyway.*

"You're right," says Dominic. "That's never a good starting point. We need to offer her our respect and our protection."

"Only because we need her," says Thorn.

I narrow my eyes. "That's not the point."

"How so?"

I run my hands through my hair. "I mean, that's not the reason we should treat her with respect."

"Caspian is right, she's earned it," says Rhys.

"From you maybe," Thorn snarls. "But we haven't even met her yet."

"Simmer down." I place a hand on my brother's shoulder. If it was a stranger touching Thorn, he might fly into a rage, but he quiets down and takes a step back.

"Fine, I'll see how everything plays out. For now." Thorn crosses the tree trunks he calls arms over his chest.

Iphigenia throws out her hands, apparently reenacting something from her show for her sister. I like her full name, it suits her. Even if she weren't a person of interest in our case, I'd still want to get to know her. The way she carries herself with such confidence, yet her eyes remain open and smiling. Rhys is already hooked. Now I can see why.

CHAPTER FOUR

IPHIGENIA

"Wow." Chrys's voice is high and breathy. "Just wow. Iphi, you were amazing. That was your best routine yet. And that fall and dismount at the end? Girl, you could easily get a job with Cirque du Soleil."

"You think?" I'm having a difficult time focusing on my sister's words, given the proximity of Rhys and his friends. And the blond one in particular, the way he's been looking at me, sends goose bumps over my body. There's a soft intensity to his gaze, more welcoming than predatory, and I can't help reacting to it.

She touches my shoulder, bringing me back, and then pulls me in for a hug. "Absolutely."

When I pull away there are actual tears in her eyes, which pings me right to my core. Her reaction adds to the guilt surging through me for being distracted by Mr. Sex Hair. She doesn't have to say a word; her pride pierces me and I can't help standing up a little straighter. I toss my head to dislodge his image and refocus.

Chrys is my oldest sister and she's been through so much. She spent the largest portion of her life drifting through Mom's shadow. Until she met her honey—who steps up and throws an arm around her shoulders.

Carter grins. "Fantastic job, Iphi."

"Thank you, and thank you both for coming. I know this wasn't easy for you."

And with that, my sister's brown eyes dart around the pier, searching the crowd still milling around the big top.

I place a hand on her shoulder. "It's okay. Mom's not here."

Carter pulls her in tighter, tucking her against his chest. "We almost didn't come, just in case. But I told Chrys that Aurelia has yet to show up to a performance. And she said—"

"—with my luck, she'll pick tonight," Chrys finishes. "But, it's more important to support you on opening night than to fear running into the big bad witch of the Edge."

She tosses her chestnut-brown hair. Tonight

she's wearing it styled in soft waves that cascade to her shoulders. I know I wasn't the only one silently rejoicing when she stopped wearing it up in a severe ponytail. Though she'd probably deck me if I told her the way she tosses it over her shoulder is pure Aurelia.

Throwing my arms around my sister and her beau, I hug both of them tightly. I'm pretty much the sole hugger in our non-touchy-feely family, but I know that everyone secretly likes it. The advantages of my gift. Both of them hug me back, Chrys a little more stiffly than Carter. But she's trying and that's what counts.

"Is Sadie here?" I say into her soft hair, releasing my hold on them.

Chrys leans away. "She and Ryder sat with us. The rest of the gang, too. Everyone loved it. You especially."

"Where are they?" I crane my neck around the crowd, searching for Sadie's siren-red hair.

"No one but us wanted to stick around in case Mom made an appearance."

That says a lot for Chrys, as she's the one most on the outs with Aurelia. I beam at her, my already soft heart oozing into jelly. Perhaps it's for the best that Mother didn't show up-again. "Thank you for staying."

She reddens prettily, smiling so big her teeth show. "You're my little sister and I'm so proud of you."

Carter waves his brother and the other men over. Rhys looks almost too good in his faded jeans and stylish button-down. Suddenly happy I remembered to grab the cape, I pull it tightly around me. Those three impossibly good-looking men flank him.

Rhys pulls his brother in for an embrace. Another hugger? Then he turns to Chrys and offers her a deep smile, clutching her hand between two of his. "So nice to see you again, Chrys."

She averts her eyes, which does nothing to mask her rising blush.

Rhys turns to me, his dark eyes boring into mine. I could lose myself in that gaze. "You were amazing."

"Thank you." I grin up at him.

Someone clears his throat and Rhys looks away. "Let me introduce you to my cousins." His voice is a deep, penetrating rumble.

I take in the other men. So they're *related* to Rhys; now their collective hotness makes sense. Each of the three are gorgeous, clearly related, and yet distinctive. Mr. Sex Hair's shoulder-length blond mane falls across his face, hiding one pale-blue eye. Even halved, the effect of his gaze is electrifying. Up pop those damn goose bumps again.

I'm almost grateful when the tallest moves toward me first, breaking my gaze with Mr. Sex Hair. I look up . . . and up. He's at least six foot three. He grasps my hand and kisses the top. He's not a beanpole either. The man is built like a pro wrestler. His arms are as big as my thighs. To top off the intimidation factor, he's completely bald, which totally works on him. "I'm Thorn Vidal, and these are my brothers," he booms. He motions to the two remaining men at his side. My admirer from afar steps forward.

"Caspian." He tucks his windswept blond hair behind his ears. Despite the blazing eye contact, everything about this one screams safe. Gentle, perceptive. Someone who looks at the world and life with wonderment. Caspian's lips turn up and he offers me the smallest of bows.

The last man steps forward and offers me his hand. "Nice to finally meet you, Iphigenia. I'm Dominic." Dominic clutches my hand for a beat. His sea-green eyes swirl with calculation under dark-blond brows and close-cropped hair. I suppress an urge to squirm. It's as though he's trying to see inside my head, to pick out my inner thoughts. If he likes what he's finding, I can't tell. Dominic's features, too, fall between those of his brothers.

The three of them possess such an intensity that I momentarily lose my words.

"That was an amazing performance," Caspian says into the quiet. His blue eyes sparkle like sunlight on a calm sea after a hurricane. "I hope you don't mind that I took some photographs." He produces a rather impressive-looking digital camera, then steps to my side to show me the back screen. I gasp at the photos he's captured of me—in midair.

"Are you a professional photographer?"

His head bows, eyes not meeting mine, as he fiddles with some camera buttons. "Amateur."

I place a hand on his arm. "Well I'm no expert, but these look professional to me. I know Serlon would love to see them if you're looking to sell any."

His head shakes rapidly. "Not these, but I'd be happy to take some others for him, no charge."

I giggle. "You shouldn't give your art away for free."

"We're all gainfully employed," Thorn says. "Photography is Caspian's hobby."

"I see. I haven't seen any of you here before."

"We just moved to the Edge," says Dominic.

"For?" I ask, blatantly probing.

"Boring work stuff," he responds. "But we'd rather talk about you."

"Me?" The hairs on the back of my neck prickle.

"What my brother means," says Caspian, "is that we're more interested in learning about you than we are in talking about ourselves."

"Why?"

Caspian's eyes widen. "Because you're a beautiful, talented, enigmatic woman."

My admirer indeed, and not the least bit shy about showing it. "So are lots of other girls in the circus." I wave my hand toward other performers milling about and talking to the crowd.

His eyes soften and he smiles. "Of course. We'll take our leave now."

But those eyes remain on me.

"It was a pleasure to meet you, Miss Holt," Thorn says. "We thoroughly enjoyed your performance." He takes my hand and kisses the top of it once again.

Each brother gives me a slight nod before they turn to go.

"Caspian," I call, and he turns back, a hopeful look in his eyes. "I'd love to see all of the photos you took, maybe get a few copies?"

He fishes in his pocket, then hands me a card with a little flourish. "Call, email, or text me, milady." With a formal bow, he joins his brothers.

"What the heck was that?" I ask Rhys, who still stands next to me.

He grins. "Admirers. Can you blame them?"

I choose to ignore his comment. "Where's Chrys?"

"She and Carter went home. They asked me to give you this." He leans in and kisses my cheek.

I jump back and turn beet red.

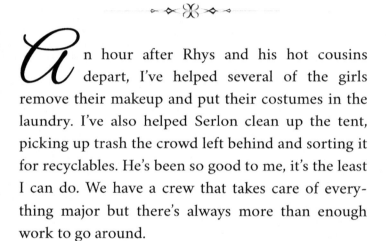

An hour after Rhys and his hot cousins depart, I've helped several of the girls remove their makeup and put their costumes in the laundry. I've also helped Serlon clean up the tent, picking up trash the crowd left behind and sorting it for recyclables. He's been so good to me, it's the least I can do. We have a crew that takes care of everything major but there's always more than enough work to go around.

One of the girls offers me a ride but the weather is so lovely that I want to walk. Home isn't too far from the boardwalk, and part of the walk is along Discovery Highway, the road that runs from one end of the Edge to the other. The water flanks it, and this is my favorite time to walk it, when I don't have to share it with crowds and traffic. The waves undulate in the moonlight. The splashing of the water kissing the rocky edge below drifts up to the road, and a barn owl hooting in the night adds to the soothing rhythm.

I walk along the highway until the turn-off, Crescent Street, to our cul-de-sac. But I'm not alone tonight. Someone is . . . moaning?

The sound carries faintly on the wind. I spin around. There's nothing other than swaying palm trees and empty yards. But the sounds are a little louder now and . . . wetter? I follow the noises to a bungalow down the street from us. There, in a darkened doorway, two figures are locked in an embrace. I almost look away again—no need to intrude on their intimacy—but something feels off. That hand, it's not gripping the other in ecstasy. It's flat, pushing. Straining. And weakening.

Stepping closer, I pull my 'vampire special' spray out which works on humans, too. Pepper spray infused with silver to keep them both at bay. Clutching it in one hand, I hold my keychain alarm in the other.

The closer I get, the louder my heart beats in my chest until I know that at least one of them can hear it, too. The creature looks up, dropping his prey, fangs wet with fresh blood. His eyes are wild and bloodshot, his hair disheveled, his face massively scarred. Though I gasp, he makes no move toward me. His victim slips to the ground, limp, curled up in a ball, and moaning.

I point the spray right at his face. "Get away from her!"

The remorseful look in those haunted eyes says it all but my entire body goes rigid with his fear. His heart races at a speed that no vampire's should, mixed with overwhelming grief. His sadness is so palpable that tears spill down my cheeks. Before he vanishes, I pick up one distinct thought: *It's you*. Then in a flash, he's gone.

What the hell?

I dart forward and drop to my knees, gathering the woman in my arms, petting her hair. "It's going to be okay. You're okay."

"What happened?" She looks up at me.

"Did you know the vampire who was drinking from you?"

"What vampire?"

Okay, that's weird. Vampires live openly in the human world, have for centuries, with willing citizens lining up to offer their veins. Sure, I've heard the tales from long ago, when they fed on unwilling victims. And though stories of rogue or renegade vampires make the paper even now, they're rare— and they're never in Distant Edge.

The woman struggles to her feet, my arm around

her shoulder keeping her steady. She shakes her head, looking around, and then back at me.

"Who are you?"

"I'm a neighbor. My name is Iphigenia Holt."

The woman pulls away but she's too wobbly to stand on her own. I grab her waist to keep her upright but she pushes me away and smacks into the doorjamb behind her.

"Evil witch, I know your kind," she snarls. "What did you do to me?"

"Nothing." I hold my hands up. "I was walking home and saw the attack, so I chased the vampire away."

She snorts. "Liar. You little liar. Your whole family is evil. Get away from me!"

"I'm not leaving until you're safely inside."

Never taking her eyes off me, the woman digs into the purse hanging on her shoulder and produces a keychain. "I'm reporting you to the police," she says, her voice groggy. "Not that they'll do anything. They're all in your back pocket, aren't they?"

I wish I could say I'm surprised, but people hate what they fear and don't understand. Others are envious of our powers to the point of anger. But I'm trying to help her and I'm obviously no threat. A long sigh escapes before I can hold it back. "I understand your anger but I've only shown you kindness. And why live in the Edge if you hate Signum so much?"

"You know why, girl." Her voice is laced with venom.

I step back and watch as she opens her front door and disappears inside. I count the click of seven locks—the number humans have been told will keep out witches. Still, I wait a few more moments, until lights blaze on in her front room.

Why does she hate me and my family so much? Aurelia never goes out of her way to endear herself to humans, but other than our old neighbor, I don't remember her tormenting anyone in the neighborhood.

This woman's right, though. I do know why she's here, and so many of the others as well. Only two kinds of humans live in the Edge: the ones who are enamored of Signum and want to live among us, and the ones who have been paid to move here. Several years after out town was founded, there were only a handful of human families. When the Council was formed, they levied a tax to gather funds to incentivize more humans to move here. The offer was hard to beat. If they moved here, their moving expenses were paid for, they got a free house, and they were given a job. So many humans wanted to move that a lottery had to be instated.

Now, this woman, like so many others, has found herself stuck here without the resources to leave. If any of the winners want to move out, they can, but they can't sell their house—because the city owns it.

I clutch my silver pepper spray can so hard the nozzle leaves an imprint in my hand, but then I remember my amulet. It's a silver-filigreed teardrop topped with a pentacle, and it packs quite a magical punch, thanks to my powerful mother. She made each of her daughters one for protection—nothing on this street can touch me while I wear it, even though I'm alone. Nevertheless, the entire walk home, I am vigilant for danger.

Logically, I know I should call the police and report the incident but after spending time in the creature's head, engulfed in his misery, I hesitate. Confusion settles over me. If I turn him in, they'll lock him up forever. Maybe I can help him. I should at least try. Talking to my vampire friend Burgundy about it first seems like the sensible next step.

I briefly consider calling Mother and asking her to meet me, but she would overreact and lock me in my room until the rogue vamp was caught. And who knows when that will be.

By the time I'm standing on my own front steps,

I'm shaking. I take deep breaths to steady myself. I cannot let Aurelia see me this way.

The door flies open and there she stands, her hands planted on her hips. "Where have you been?"

"I'm sorry, Mom. I stayed after to help some of the girls."

"You texted me an hour ago, saying you were on your way home."

"I got waylaid. A neighbor down the street needed help."

Her eyes narrow. "What neighbor and what kind of help? Are you starting to lie to me like your sisters?"

I shake my head. "No, and I don't want to talk about it." I push past her and go to my room. She starts to follow, but ever the buffer, Alistair stops her.

Wishing I could lock my door, I sit down on my bed and pull out my iPad, searching the local news sites for any stories about a rogue vampire. There's nothing I can find, but if that woman's memory loss is any indication, it doesn't mean he hasn't struck before. And what happens next time? What if he can't stop himself and he accidentally kills someone? Or worse?

CHAPTER FIVE

IPHIGENIA

a little before noon the next day, I slip down to the floor at the base of the front door and bury my face in Armageddon's soft fur. He purrs and butts me with his head, emitting soft mewls that he reserves for no one else.

"Shhh, big guy," I whisper and he immediately stops. "I'll be back soon." He pushes against my arm, rubbing his face over me, but steps back when I rise to let myself out.

Like so many animals I've met, Army would follow me to the ends of the earth. "Beast whisperer" people sometimes call me behind my back. Not very original, if you ask me.

I take a different route through our neighborhood to reach the highway. I do *not* want to run into Ms. Angry Pants Human this morning. The breeze off the ocean whistles through the trees. The branches of the cypress trees growing along the water's edge stretch toward the bay like an aerialist's fingertips reaching for her ribbon. It's easy to block out the sounds of traffic and focus instead on the hypnotic rhythm of the waves.

Once I reach the boardwalk, I spot Rex before I spot Burgundy. I bound toward the Rottweiler, throwing my arms around him, and burying my face in his short fur. The beast licks my face.

Burgundy laughs. "Sometimes I thinks he likes you better than me."

"Not a chance." I stand up and take a seat next to him. "You're his mama. I'm just an auntie."

Already piled on the table is a plate of half-eaten bacon, bread, and coffee. One of Burgundy's greatest joys is eating human food, and she has the curves to prove it. The vampire describes herself as Rubenesque or full-figured, but I have always called her beautiful.

I wait until after ordering myself breakfast and getting coffee to tell her about the vampire attack the night before. The entire time I'm speaking, her expression morphs from incredulous to pissed to worried. "Have you ever heard of anything like that?" I finish.

She bites her plump lower lip, sawing it between

her teeth, and lets out a long breath. "I've heard tales, rumors really, but if what you saw happens on a regular basis and it's not witnessed, it's no surprise that it goes under the radar."

"Do you possess this kind of ability?" I ask point-blank.

She looks away and then grabs a piece of bread, slathering it with butter. After she takes a bite and chews it for a moment, she nods.

I wait until she's swallowed before raising my eyebrows at her.

"There are a great many hormones and chemicals that we can inject into our prey."

I gasp, covering my mouth a beat too late.

She drops the bread on her plate. "Sorry, Iph. It's how vamps often refer to humans when they're not in earshot. No need to take offense." She offers me an enigmatic smile. "Think of it as a compliment that it slipped out with you."

"Go on." I lean back as the waiter places my omelet in front of me. In front of Burgundy, he places french toast, piled high with whipped cream and strawberries. Her second breakfast of the morning, by the looks of it.

"Gotta keep up my figure." She winks at me. "Gives my lovers more of me to fight over. Tiyah enjoys my boobs and Elijah fancies himself an ass man."

I roll my eyes and giggle. "You were saying . . ."

"We do have a compound in our venom that makes our prey forget. Most vampires never use it because we don't have to. And well, as you know, especially in the Edge, such chemicals are illegal to inject."

"But it's there for a reason."

"It is, like so many other archaic practices." She cuts a piece of her candy toast and pushes it into her mouth.

"It was used when there were no willing victims?"

"Back in the day," she says around her food.

"Wouldn't evolution have removed that need then?"

Swallowing, Burgundy reaches for her coffee and takes a sip. "From what I understand, evolution takes a very long time to catch up. Truth be told, I've used it on occasion as well, not for that reason, but for others."

"So it's still accessible because it's still used." A statement, not a question.

She shrugs. "Did you tell Sheldon about this?"

I shake my head before she's finished the question, though unable to say why exactly.

"Well you need to report it."

"Are you sure?"

"Yes, Iphi, no question. Hey." She lifts my chin with a finger. "I know you're a bleeding heart and I love you for that, but we don't know what we're dealing with here. This guy could be totally dangerous and hurt more innocent people. Maybe even kill someone accidentally. I know you don't want that on your conscience."

"You're right," I sigh and look away, blinking rapidly to hide the tears.

"Can you describe him to the cops?"

Oh, yes, that face haunted me all night. "Maybe it was just a one-time thing or he was passing through on his way elsewhere."

"Regardless, you're reporting this." She dabs at her lips with a napkin. "I'll come with."

❧ ❖ ❀ ❖ ❧

It's a lovely walk to the police station at the center of town and if Rex could talk, he'd thank us for it. When the breeze billows off the water, it sets my hair adrift, tickling my neck and ears. Rex turns his face into it and opens his mouth, a pink tongue lolling out.

The architecture downtown is a historic throwback to the times of the Californian gold rush mixed with a Southwestern flavor, some neoclassical flair, and all of it giving off a distinctly beachy vibe. But instead of looking like a rowdy mishmash, each building flows harmoniously into the next. Next to the neoclassical city hall, the police station is an orange-yellow adobe building with a terra cotta roof.

The police chief's office is to the right of the great lobby and we wait outside for an officer on duty to announce our arrival.

"Burgundy, Iphigenia," the chief says, ushering us in.

Chief Sheldon is a large, intimidating man and if I hadn't known him for years, I'd be shaking in my flip-flops. His salt-and-pepper hair is thinning, but it only makes his thick mustache look darker. Why do so many cops have mustaches? Last year he didn't need glasses, but now he wears a pair on his nose.

We sit down while he moves to the other side of his desk and Rex lies down at our feet. "Burgundy said you had something to tell me?" He cocks his head at me, those piercing cop eyes holding my gaze through his wire-rimmed specs.

Wetting my lips, I quickly recount what I witnessed. He's shaking his head during most of it.

"Thank you for coming here," he says when I'm

done. "I do not like the sound of this, a rogue vampire that can't heal his own wounds."

"I assume that's why he can't find a donor," Burgundy adds.

"Or he just likes attacking innocent people. Regardless, this is worrisome." Sheldon looks at me. "And I'm concerned for your safety."

"What? Why?"

"You got a good look at him; he knows you got a good look at him. He may come after you, if for no other reason than to wipe your memory."

"Which is why we're here now," Burgundy says. "Do you have a sketch artist or can you call one from San Diego County?"

"We have one. He's new." Sheldon picks up his phone and fires off a text. Less than a minute later, there's a knock on his door and then it opens.

I have to hold my hand over my mouth to keep from gasping. It's Caspian—with a Distant Edge Police Department staff ID card hanging from his belt.

"Iphigenia." He's instantly at my side. "Is everything okay?"

"Iphi witnessed a vampire attack last night," says the chief. "Take her to an interview room for a sketch of the perp."

He touches my arm. "Are you okay?"

"Well, hello there," purrs Burgundy. She gets to her feet beside Caspian. "I'm Burgundy." The woman can't help flirting with every gorgeous man and woman she meets. It's in her nature. So why do I want to claw her eyes out?

"Ma'am." Caspian nods toward her, his gaze never leaving mine. He takes my elbow and leads me out of the room, holding a hand up to keep her and Rex from following. I wish I could snap a pic of the look on her face.

On our way to the back of the station, I engage my elbow holder, trying to figure out why he's here. "So, you're a cop?" *Gold medal for lamest question of the day, Iphigenia.*

He barks out a laugh and lets go of my elbow but doesn't respond. "Civilian, actually. But I do work here."

I've never been to this part of the station before. A whole raft of officers are working away at their desks. Are these the ones who never get to leave and make rounds? It's a large room with the desks all set up together like in every cop movie and television show I've ever seen. No cubicles. No privacy. Does squishing everyone together foster camaraderie?

I do a double take when I spot Caspian's brothers here, too. Dominic sits behind a computer, leaning forward to focus on his screen while the imposing Thorn stands behind him with an open manila folder. Dominic has an ID card like Caspian's hanging from a lanyard around his neck, but Thorn has an actual badge on his belt. At some point, my escort pulled ahead of me. Caspian is waiting by a far door, suppressing a bemused smile. Great. I hurry to catch up.

"Your whole family works here?" I whisper, standing on my tiptoes.

"Everyone but Rhys." He opens the door for me and ushers me into a small room. I always imagined what an interrogation room would look like and this is not it. The tiny room has a wooden table in the center and two padded chairs, one on each side. My first thought is that this can't be where they bring criminals because those chairs would make great weapons. Okay, crazy thoughts, be gone. Nerves much?

Maybe this isn't an interrogation room at all, or maybe our town is too small to have those two-may mirrors I've seen on television. Sheldon *did* call it an "interview" room. Is there a difference?

Caspian motions for me to sit and moves the other chair next to mine. Crossing the room to a side table, he removes a pitcher of water and two paper cups stacked on top of each other and brings them over. He pours the water for me and then sits down.

"Ready?" He opens up the sketchpad that's already on the table and picks up one of those blue artist pencils Chrys uses.

I close my eyes and try to recall everything I can.

"That's good, you're already doing what I was going to tell you to do. Try to form a snapshot in your mind of the person you saw and let's start with the shape of his face."

I take a deep inhale to fill my lungs, then hold it, conjuring. Letting it out, I begin.

Less than thirty minutes later, Caspian shows me the sketch. While I was speaking, I'd assumed he would show me what he was drawing and I would correct certain aspects, but either that's not how he works or there was no need. The image is near perfect, akin to his photographs.

"Have you always been an artist?" I ask.

"Yeah. My interest in photography is more recent, though." He ducks his head, smudging something on the page with his thumb. "There's something that draws me to it. Plus, I equate drawing with work now."

His broad smile reaches his captivating eyes. I could fall into those eyes and lose myself. Now where did that come from? Aren't I attracted to Rhys?

"Iphigenia?" Caspian is staring at me.

"Yes?" I peer at him, unsuccessfully trying not to blush because even though he's hiding it, he's attracted to me. Unlike his brothers, Caspian's emotions are painted all over his face. Probably because he's a sensitive artist, like Chrys. Even if I weren't an empath, I could have figured him out easy.

"My brothers and I are concerned about your safety."

"How do they know what happened?"

Caspian's gaze darts behind me. "I texted them. It's our civic duty to protect the citizens of the Edge."

Great, that's all I am to them, just another denizen of the Edge. What else would I be? They're practically strangers. I stand up, turning toward the door. "I appreciate that, and I understand that as an officer it's your job, but I relinquish you of that duty. I've gone my whole life without any escorts. That vampire couldn't have attacked me last night even if he'd wanted to, and he didn't. I'm not afraid." It's true. I'm not afraid. I want Caspian and his brothers to like me for me, not because they think I'm some weakling who needs their protection. As if.

Caspian

"*W*ait, please."

She pauses with her hand on the door handle, keeping her back to me.

So much about this woman confuses me, but she's hiding something. I just don't know what. Either she's far more intuitive than anyone I've ever met or she's using a mind-reading spell or something.

She wants to be on her own, she's made that much clear. But the easy, relaxed performer of last night is gone. Instead, the whole time she's been here, she's been holding herself straight, her eyes watchful and sober, as if anticipating trouble. There's a thread of fear underneath it all, one she's hiding even from herself.

"You're not invincible." And when I think about what could have happened last night, it's all I can do not to throw my arms around her.

"I know." Her shoulders droop. Then she clears her throat. "Thank you for your concern, Caspian. I get that you're worried about me. I really do. But I have this amulet." She turns to face me, holding up a small silver pendant. "It protects me from harm."

The firm set of her jaw tells me it's fruitless to argue with her. "Fine. But please be careful."

She gives me a quick nod, her eyes softening, before she heads out.

Why does this woman intrigue the hell out of me? She's different from any woman I've ever met. Maybe it's because she's such a dichotomy. Strong and capable, probably the strongest woman I've ever met. Yet so vulnerable.

Since we moved here, it's been mostly my job to keep an eye on her. My brothers and I have been tracking the rogue vamp across the country for a while. Almost a year now. Then a beat cop came across the vampire's belongings during a sweep of a tent city in Seattle two months back. A photo of Iphigenia was nestled among his stuff. When all signs of the rogue disappeared afterward, the photo was our only clue to his next move. Facial recognition databases of the girl turned up nothing—not surprising after getting to know this mighty sunbeam. She may be hiding something but she's certainly no criminal. Nor did those tools turn up any matches from social media sites. Signum rarely hang out on Facebook, after all. Why make it easy for the angry, pitchfork-wielding villagers to find your doorstep?

No, instead, it was sheer, unmitigated luck when

Rhys's half-brother Carter sent him a photo. A photo of their Grandpa Alistair with his new girlfriend and her daughter.

We were on the phone to the Edge's police department the next day, offering the chief our services. The moment we hit town, surveillance began in earnest.

Day and night, Iphigenia stops for every animal that crosses her path. Kneeling and cooing to them until she can read their tags and return them to their owners. If they're strays, she sneaks them food and water out of her mother's house. She'll sit and pet the mangiest of creatures, strays other people ignore, turning their noses up into the air—or worse, kicking them in the rump.

She's not even afraid of a rogue vampire that obviously wants her for nefarious reasons. How can someone so tiny in stature be so large in spirit? I finger the sketch in front of me. God, this will kill Rhys.

We've all taken turns surveilling her, waiting for the rogue to appear, but I've pulled watcher duty the most. For one, because I'm good with a camera. And for another, I have more expendable working hours. Rhys hustles from job to job, trying to save up enough money or gather enough students for his future dojo. Dom and Thorn work long shifts at the station. But Chief Sheldon rarely needs his departmental sketch artist at a moment's notice. Except for today. But then, I was already here, dying to know why she was in with the chief.

When I found out, I wanted to kick myself. Bad enough she ran into the rogue, but where the rogue goes, worse things follow. We should have been on her last night, but since she'd just been introduced to us, we thought it best to hang back on a night she would almost certainly be going home with family or a coworker. We are idiots. But then again, is it just a coincidence that the rogue found her on a night we weren't there?

A moment later, there's a soft knock on the door. Must be the boss wanting my sketch. I rip it out of my book and start neatening up. "Come in."

The door clicks opens and Iphigenia stands there, biting her lip.

My entire body tightens, ready to spring to her aid. "Is everything okay?"

She walks into the room and perches back in the chair next to me and my body relaxes. I let out the air I was holding in my lungs.

"I was wondering . . ." She worries her hands, looking away and then back again.

I wait silently, giving her some space.

"Do you have any photographs you've taken? On your phone?"

I was not expecting that question. "Of what?"

"Anything. I want to see some of your work."

Unexpected, but I'm so relieved she's not in immediate distress. "Sure." I take out my phone and click to the folder that contains some of my more innocuous work, then hand it over to her.

She's silent while she flips through the first couple, which are, admittedly, not that great. Then she comes to a stop on one of my favorites, a cloudscape.

"That's amazing. The way you captured the light in those clouds really sets a mood." She raises her head. "You're very talented."

"Thank you."

Iphigenia turns back to my phone, swiping through the next few, stopping and staring at each one before moving forward. "I'm sorry I was so short with you. I know you're coming from a caring place," she says without looking up.

I want to reach out and clasp her hand but I don't.

After a moment she stops and lets out an "Awwwww." I lean in to see her stopped on a photo that Dominic took of me in my large shift.

"I love cats," she purrs. "Even big ones."

Smiling, I lean in closer. Should I tell her it's me?

"He's so majestic. Obviously he's a predator, but the light shining in those eyes denotes far too much benevolence. This must be a shifter, caught in his shift. Yes?" She meets my gaze, licking her plump-raspberry lips and I have a sudden compulsion to kiss her.

She startles, jumping backward, the wheels of her chair scraping along the linoleum floor. "I gotta go." She stands up and drops my phone on the table. Without another word, she rushes out of the room.

CHAPTER SIX

IPHIGENIA

I'm working out at home when my phone buzzes. Grabbing my cell, I blink several times and reread the text. Rhys and his brothers—er, cousins, want to take me to dinner? Mother is already cooking, and her distress over a late cancellation may very well overwhelm both her system and mine. And that's without the added nerves from seeing Caspian again. I can't hold it against him that he wanted to kiss me. It's not like he was actually going to do it, and if I weren't an empath, I'd never have known. Plus, dammit, he's cute. That long, sandy-blond hair, those eyes that blaze under dark-blond lashes. The color reminds me of a blanket of fog hovering over a sea burning up in the early morning sunlight. Stop thinking about Caspian.

How about dessert? I text back.

Sounds good. I'll pick you up. What time?

No, thank you, I'd rather walk.

Not with a renegade vampire on the loose. I'll be there at 9pm.

Great. Aurelia's going to kill me and then he can take a corpse to dessert. Still, I don't want to let on that I'm a twenty-year-old woman with a career and yet still living under my mother's very heavy thumb. My choice. I'll just have to make her understand.

After finishing my workout I get ready for dinner. Mother always serves at seven each and every night. Like clockwork.

I pile my corkscrew curls on top of my head with a heap of bobby pins strategically placed in order to hide them. I change into a summer dress, nothing too fancy, and throw on a pair of kitten heels.

Waiting until dinner so that Alistair is present as a buffer before I broach the subject may not have been the best strategy.

"Don't you look lovely," he says as I take my seat at the table, which is already laden with food.

"Why are you all dressed up?" Mother sniffs. "You don't have a performance tonight, do you?"

She knows perfectly well that I don't. "Rhys is picking me up at nine. We're going out for dessert."

"Rhys?" Aurelia's eyes narrow. "Without my permission?"

"Darling," Alistair reaches a hand over to pat her arm, "Iphigenia is a grown woman, and my grandson is quite honorable. I'm happy to see them getting along."

"Is that what you call it?" she hisses. "Getting along? More like trying to get into my daughter's pants."

"Mother!" I keep my tone stern. "We're going to Confections for dessert, not eloping. I barely know him. Please give me more credit than that."

She tosses her thick mane over one shoulder. "Well," she concedes, "you aren't like your loose sisters."

My poor sisters still get the brunt of mother's condemnation. Sadie, our middle sister, had a sex witch for a father and thus, through no fault of her own but much to Aurelia's dismay, is also a sex witch. A sesso. She needs to be charged up sexually for her magic to work. Luckily, she found Ryder—the yang to her yin. And then there's Chrys, who Mother always thought would remain at home forever to take care of her. Chrys, the late bloomer who bloomed enough to leave us all and move in with Carter.

"Chrysothemis was never loose, Mom," I press, "and Sadie can't help who she is. It hurts me"—I press my hand to my chest where the pain blossoms white-hot—"when you disrespect them like that."

"What should hurt you, my dearest one, is the foul way they treat their own mother."

"I want everyone in our family to get along." Why can't I just let this go like usual?

"As do I," Alistair agrees.

"And I want your sisters to be more like you," Mother says, looking at me. "But life doesn't work that way, does it?"

Poor Mother. She holds her past heartaches close, but she's been hurt so deeply that she created a hard outer shell to protect herself from more pain. People hate Mother, openly hate her, and I understand that, too. She can be harsh and unyielding but what they don't see is the ferocity of her love.

I remember when Father disappeared. I was only six. I woke up from a horrific nightmare: Father screaming our names, pounding and kicking while enclosed in the grasp of a giant beast. It was before I knew what I was, and the terror that seized and squeezed my heart was almost too painful for me to bear. Like a hot poker stabbing me in my chest, over and over again.

That night, I ran into the living room, crying. "Iphigenia, what's the matter?" Mother asked.

"It's Daddy," I cried, throwing myself on top of

her. And even though she wasn't a touchy-feely mom, she wrapped her arms around me, enclosing me in her warmth.

Breathing hard against my hair, she cried with me, her tears splashing against my cheek. "I'm here and I'm not going anywhere."

But as comforting as her arms were, my pain only wound hers tighter. Soon, it was too much to bear and I struggled out of her grasp, running to my room, where I threw myself on my bed and sobbed for hours. Mother put her own emotions aside to comfort me again, crawling onto my bed and holding me. Stoic in her pain, sponging up mine as if she knew just how to give back to an empath.

This is the Aurelia no one sees, the one who devoted herself to her children after my father left. The strong woman who kept our family together, pushing down her own fears, stamping out her own depression and abandonment issues. There was something else, too. Our mother had a past, other children, another husband, long ago. But no one else knows. Only me. All of those locked-up memories and emotions make it difficult for others to empathize with the hard, cold exterior Aurelia presents to the world.

"I won't stay out too late but I am going to Confections with Rhys tonight. I hope you'll give me your blessing to do so." I reach for the mashed potatoes while Alistair pats my mother's arm.

Though I'd rather not lie, sometimes I have to. More often, I choose to withhold, which I still consider a form of lying. Deceit by omission. With Aurelia, I'm deceptive so she won't be hurt. That's what I tell myself, anyway. No need for her to know about the earlier vampire attack and have her worry and helicopter-parent me even more than she already does. No need to tell her that Rhys's three cop cousins will be at Confections, too. Would that set her mind at ease or would she think they all wanted to gang-bang me? Probably the latter. For a woman so old-fashioned and uptight, she sure does think the worst of others. But, I remind myself, she's seen so much in her past. And she only worries about me because she cares so much.

"That's lovely," Alistair adds into the pregnant silence, twirling the handlebar mustache he's grown out to please my mother. "Rhys needs friends here."

"Friends," she scoffs, "is that what the kids are calling lovers these days?"

"Mother." I stand up from the table. "I've done nothing wrong. Please do not make me regret telling you of my plans tonight. I'm an adult and I do not have to ask your permission."

"While under my roof, you most certainly do."

Placing my hands on my hips, I stand my ground, knowing that the last thing she wants is for me to move out, but she says nothing.

"Would you prefer I stay with Sadie for a while?"

"No. Of course not." She helps herself to some green beans, remembering, no doubt, when I stayed with Sadie for months last year. "Sit down. And please don't stay out too late."

Rhys

I ring the bell at exactly nine o'clock. But my smile slips when Aurelia throws the front door open, not Iphigenia. The woman stands in front of me straighter than the broomstick in her hands. Her hair, which is normally a strawberry blond, has darkened to a bloodred and is actually whirling around her face, caught in a nonexistent wind. I look down at her feet and smother a chuckle. Here is a witch with untold power, and she's using it to intimidate a man she fears is trying to date her daughter. And . . . she's not wrong.

The chuckle dies in my throat.

I would indeed love to date Iphi, but that's not why I'm here. My first priority is the welfare of my family and the town. To prevent or mitigate the horrors coming. Perhaps the queen witch of the Edge has picked up on this. My eyes do not meet hers, as if she can see my ulterior motives merely by looking at me.

"What are your intentions toward my daughter?" she spits out.

"Good evening to you, Ms. Holt. You look lovely as always." I hold out my hand but she gives me the stink eye, refusing to take it.

"Rhys, wonderful to see you, chap." Alistair hurries over, patting me on the shoulder. A moment later, Iphi appears and my heart bounces in my chest like a rubber ball. She looks absolutely stunning, of course. Her hair is piled on top of her head in an elegant, intricate updo, emphasizing a long neck that begs to be nibbled on. Yet I can't help wondering what her hair would look like down. Like a mermaid's or a woodland nymph's. Something natural. Not tamed or forced into a smooth façade so unlike her true personality. I want her to let it fly, wild and free, whenever she wishes. I want her to embrace her passionate nature instead of forcing herself into the obedience her mother so obviously demands.

Her cat mewls at her feet, pushing his face into her leg. Iphi drops to the floor, sitting next to the cat, and it crawls into her lap. She lowers her head as they rub their faces together, both of them with closed eyes. It's too fucking adorable. Lucky cat.

My jealousy of the animal is sudden, bitter, and wholly unconnected to my physical attraction for her. How different would things have turned out if I'd had a little Iphi in my neighborhood, doling out daily hugs to the feral strays me and Nolan and my cousins were?

My playboy father left when I was still crawling, and my mother died right after Nolan was born, too beaten down by life and her choice in men to keep going.

Carter tried to help me and Nolan, but his mother didn't want anything to do with two orphaned hellions, much less crossbreeds. When Thorn found out how abysmally we were being treated, he insisted on taking us in even though Thorn, all of fourteen years old at the time, was already feeding and raising Caspian and Dominic, plus himself. Still, he never looked at me as a burden or another kid to watch over.

Probably because Thorn and Dom remembered the idyllic life their parents had given them. Caspian was six when they were killed, so he doesn't remember nearly as much. Maybe it's better that way; he certainly seems happier for it. He never really knew what he was missing. Spending his formative years growing up on the streets with me and Nolan and his brothers, thinking that's how life was supposed to be, made him even more adaptable.

As if Iphi realizes both her mother and I are standing there, watching her, she scoops the cat up into her arms and stands, presenting him to me.

I freeze. It's one massive black cat. I have no idea how it'll react to . . . what I am.

"Armageddon, meet Rhys. Rhys, this is Army. He's my little love."

"There is nothing little about that cat." I dredge up a smile, and she giggles, setting him down on the floor with Aurelia tsking behind her.

"Goodnight, Mama." She leans over to peck her mother on the cheek. "Night, Al. Don't you two do anything I wouldn't do and don't wait up for me." She slips by her mother and links her arm with mine, which immediately sends a rush of warmth down my spine.

Alistair chuckles. "Cute, Iphi. We'll be good."

"We most certainly will be waiting up for you," Aurelia huffs.

Iphi is pulling my arm, practically dragging me down the driveway.

She makes an adorable sound when she sees my

car. It's halfway between a squeal and a hiccough. "That's your car? For real?"

I lead her to the passenger side and open the door for her in answer.

"A freaking pale-yellow Thunderbird? Oh my god. It's gorgeous." She slides in and I close the door.

I love my car, but I would never have called it "gorgeous" before she sat in it. After I get in on my side, I lean over. "It becomes you."

"This is literally my dream car." She clips the seat belt in, leans back, and looks at me with genuine awe.

I only wish that look was aimed at me, not at my car, but I'll take what I can get right now.

CHAPTER SEVEN

IPHIGENIA

"*C*onfections is close enough to walk," I say, trying not to ogle him in his all-black attire. Why do so many vampires wear all black? Or red, like Burgundy? They aren't creatures of the night. Do they want to be?

"Maybe I wanted to show off my cool car. Earn some brownie points."

I grin. The interior is a creamy white leather, pale and soft, like the inside of a shell after it's been tumbled through the waves. Even part of the steering wheel is white and so is the dash. White and chrome. Wow.

"Did it work?"

"Take the top down and I may concede."

Punching a button, the top slides open and I lose my train of thought yet again. The front door to the house opens and I already know what Aurelia is going to say.

"Quick, get me out of here," I stage-whisper and he complies, starting the engine, and taking me away from the prying eyes of the ever-watchful mother hen.

"Why don't you have a show tonight?" He quickly peeks over at me.

"We only have four shows a week during the summer season plus one matinee."

"Is that due to attendance? Most people don't want to go out on a weeknight?"

"Precisely." I nod. "We perform on the weekend evenings with a Sunday matinee but during the week we only have two shows. They're the least popular."

"Why isn't the circus open all year round?"

I shake my head. "A question I've been asking for years."

"And?"

"Serlon insists that when the kiddies are back in school, no one will come to the circus but I think the real reason is because he likes to winter in the Caribbean."

"Maybe you could run it during the winter?"

I wish.

There's a small parking lot next to Confections, a

sweet shop, that opened downtown a few months ago. It was started by a vampire with a sweet tooth, much like Burg. And since most vampires who indulge are plus-sized, it boasts body-positive affirmations with humor. "Love your booty, we do!" and "If you've got it, flaunt it." Then there's my favorite: "Those stares are because you're gorgeous . . . get used to it."

Rhys jumps out and opens the door for me before I can. Again.

"More brownie points," I say, and he links arms with me and leads me inside.

At a booth near the back, the three Vidal brothers are already seated. There's one space left in the booth and a chair pulled up at the end of the table. I make my way toward the chair but Rhys shakes his head and points to the booth.

Sliding in next to Caspian, I smile at each brother in turn, marveling again at how alike, yet different they all are. Dominic and Thorn sit across from me, and Rhys takes the chair.

"What would you like for dessert?" Rhys asks. It's a sweet shop but you have to go up to the counter and order, then bring your own delight back to your table.

I rub my hands together in excitement. They have everything you could ever want here, all home-made. When they first opened, I planned to work my way through the menu one tasty treat at a time. That didn't work, though. First of all, I didn't have a huge sweet tooth to begin with, and second, once I tasted their upside-down chocolate cake, I didn't want to try anything else.

"What are you guys getting?"

"How about we each get something different and we all share?" says Dominic.

Thorn rolls his eyes. "You would say that."

Ignoring him, Dominic says to me, "Is there anything you don't like?"

"What's not to like?" Caspian pats me on the back.

"Walnuts or graham cracker crust or . . . anything?" says Dominic.

I shake my head vigorously, causing several painstakingly pinned curls to fly loose.

"Too cute," says Thorn, "and a girl after my own heart. Bring it on, boys."

My jaw starts to drop but I clamp it shut. Do these men openly flirt with all women? I can't be the one bringing this out in them. I glance at Caspian and Rhys but they give no indication that they're annoyed, so why not enjoy it? *Just don't get used to it, Iphi. This is not how the real world works.*

They give their orders to Rhys, who doesn't even

write them down. I have no idea how he's going to remember everything, especially after I add my coveted upside-down chocolate cake to the list. "Be right back," he says, moving to the counter.

"So . . ." I look at the men, pausing on each ruggedly handsome face. "Why'd you all wanna meet me here?"

Thorn clears his throat, exchanging glances with the others. "Let's wait until Rhys gets back before we answer that question."

I shift in my seat. What's he hiding? "Okay then. How are all of you working for the police department? What's up with that?"

Dominic snorts but turns his eyes toward Thorn without answering.

"We all went into law enforcement because of," he licks his lips and looks at his brothers, "an unfortunate incident with our parents."

"Oh." I put my hand to my mouth. "I'm so sorry, I didn't mean to bring up anything painful." The group's agony is so palpable I shift in my seat to keep from bolting.

"It's okay." Caspian rubs my back, a quick but tender caress that sends little sparks of heat down my spine. "It was a very long time ago."

"Trackers," says Thorn.

I nod, holding up a hand. "You needn't say more."

The Trackers are a group of crazed anti-Signum zealots who gave themselves that name because they track down Signum and kill them. They murdered our friend Jared's parents and so many others. Trackers are proud to destroy the lives of the innocent, believing that all supernatural beings are inherently evil. Their logic is archaic and their lies are built on a perverted form of religion.

"We each have our own focus. Caspian, as you already know, is an amazing sketch artist."

"That he is." I smile at the man sitting next to me. Is he blushing? "But what made you guys move here in the first place?"

More loaded glances, and then Dominic clears his throat. "Our brother Rhys was moving here."

I brush a curl out of my eye. "How is he one of your brothers?"

"It's honorary," says Caspian. "We grew up together. Technically, he's a cousin but . . ."

"He's more like a brother to us," finishes Dominic. "And after he moved here to be closer to Carter, we talked Sheldon into hiring us."

"And who wouldn't want to relocate to the original Signum hotbed?" says Thorn. "But we all have different fortes, interests, even shifts."

There's obviously more to all of this and I could pry but I respect their need for privacy. They're cops, after all. Maybe it has something to do with a confidential case. "Shifters," I say aloud, trying it on. A vampire and his three shifter brothers slash cousins? How odd. But how can they be blood related? "So you and Rhys aren't really cousins then."

More glances around the table, and then Caspian speaks up. "We are, though no one really understands how exactly. Rhys's mother was a shifter and his father was a vampire."

"But cross-breeding is physically impossible!" I blurt. If I thought they were lying to me, I'd leave, but I don't sense deception from any of them. Whatever they were told, they believe it.

Caspian shrugs. "A warlock made it possible."

"Crossbreeds," I whisper, shaking my head. Who would have thought? "Does that mean Rhys can shift, too?"

Each of the brothers looks down at the table. That'd be a yes.

Caspian

Rhys comes back with a sweet-laden tray and passes the desserts out among the five of us. Then he sits at the head of the table and

Iphigenia turns to him expectantly, her bright-blue eyes batting.

"Take a bite and pass it to your right but keep your fork," he says with a smile that lights up his rugged face in a way I've never seen before.

My cousin is good-looking, gentlemanly, and interesting; many women have thrown themselves at his feet. We've all had our share, actually, but Rhys and Thorn get the most attention. I assume because they're both so domineering. And built.

Yet of all the women I've seen him with, Rhys has never looked at any of them the way he looks at Iphigenia. And it doesn't take Dom's psychology degree to figure out why. You wouldn't know it to look at him, but Rhys has not had an easy life. None of us have, but he was forced to grow up faster than most.

Iphigenia's looking at Rhys now the exact way I wish she would look at me, but it's not jealousy working its way up my spine. Rhys and I truly are as close as brothers. We've shared food, homes . . . and women.

Iphi takes a bite of her cake, pausing to lick every crumb off her fork. It would be brazen, except she has absolutely no idea what she's doing to us. The woman is merely enjoying her food. But every one of us has paused over our own plates, eyes fixated on her mouth.

I clear my throat, trying to send some blood back into my brain. "That dessert looks great, Iphigenia. Can I try a bite?"

Her head swivels toward me, her eyes peeking up at me through those thick, pale lashes. A little jolt of electricity pings through my system and I'm pretty sure it's not *just* sexual attraction. There's something so completely different about her.

Watching her on those silks, anyone can see how strong she is, both physically and psychologically. No one can do that without intense inner training and discipline. But there's also a fragility about her, one that's apparent in the way she interacts with animals and even with us. The way she reacted to the photo of me in my lion shift was with an innate understanding and acceptance of my inner beast. With love, even. Maybe I'm reading too much into it, blinded by her beauty and compassion.

Still, it's easy to see she knows we're hiding something and has chosen not to push us. Because she's trusting? She has the ability to find the best in anyone, even rogue vampires. That quality is both endearing and terrifying.

But whether she knows it or not, she's not alone anymore. I may not be a martial arts master like

Rhys. I'm certainly not a solid rock like Thorn. I'm not even a fast thinker and talker like Dominic, who can size up any situation in an instant and know how to diffuse it. But I am fast and I am agile. I've won more than a few fights by leaping around an opponent until he tires and then punching him once in the face. Maybe I don't look like a raging bull, but that doesn't mean I can't fight when it's needed.

Iphigenia takes another bite of her cake, holding eye contact with me as she does so, her tongue darting out to lick the fork. My pants tighten instantly and I hide a shiver. Her cheeks pinken as though she can read my thoughts and she looks away.

She passes the plate, as do the rest of us, but as soon as Rhys's treat appears in front of her, she becomes distracted, hovering over it.

We all go back to the desserts before us. Soon, everyone's mouth is full and one or two of my brethren are actually groaning aloud. Iphigenia stifles a giggle and digs into her own plate. Her eyes roll back in her head as she tastes Rhys's go-to treat, a warmed apple fritter. Now she's the one who's groaning.

After another bite of our desserts, we lean back in our seats, eyes trained on Thorn, our pack leader. He fell naturally into the role when we were kids.

Unlike werewolves, shifters don't usually have pack leaders. For us, it's more of an organic title. And Thorn wears it well. A weighty silence fills the air, punctuating the sounds from other tables. Teenage girls titter while their dates cajole.

"Iphigenia," Thorn says.

She leans forward. "Yes?"

"We've been told about the unfortunate incident you witnessed last night."

She bats the comment away with a wave of her hand. "It wasn't that big of a deal."

"Oh, but it was," he says, and we all nod in agreement. "It's not the first time this particular vampire has struck here and it won't be the last." He looks at Rhys, whose eyes dart away. *Could you be more obvious, man?*

"How do you know that?" she asks.

"We're cops," says Dominic, "and we have our methods."

Nice cover.

"Do you know who it is?" Iphigenia asks.

"We have an idea," Thorn answers.

"And his reasons?"

"Yes, we think we know his motivations as well. He may not have any choice," says Dominic.

"Everyone has a choice, no?"

"Not those who lack free will," says Thorn.

"Or those who are cursed," Dominic adds.

"Or are being extorted." Thorn again.

"Or controlled." Rhys finally enters the conversation.

She plops her elbows on the table. "Controlled against their will?"

"It's just one theory," says Rhys, but he won't look at her.

I sit on my hands to keep from slamming them on the table. This is ridiculous. The woman needs to know what we know. The rogue is bad enough, but it's what follows that terrifies me. The strange illnesses, the disappearances, the shattered lives. What's the purpose of keeping her in the dark? But since Thorn is technically in charge, I keep my mouth shut. It's not easy.

"Excuse me." Iphigenia leans to the side, pushing her way out of the booth.

"Where are you going?" I scoot out, too, ready to follow.

"The restroom." She looks around at the others but settles her eyes on Thorn. "Is that permitted?" Then without waiting for a response, she leaves.

"Shit, man, this is not going well." Rhys runs his hands through his hair.

"She seems to be the least guarded with Caspian."

Dominic's eyes blaze at Thorn. "Can we agree to let him take the lead when she returns?"

Yes, please. Let me rescue us from this idiocy.

Rhys inclines his head. "I think that's a great idea. I vote yes."

Thorn crosses his massive arms over his massive chest, nostrils flaring. "Fine, but I don't like it."

"You want what's best for her, yes?" I ask.

The men grumble and then shut up and force smiles on their faces at her return.

Eyes trained on me, she slips back into the booth. I keep my face soft and smile hard at her. She offers me a tiny smile in return.

"Iphigenia," I start. "We need your help." Best to appeal to her giving nature.

She chews on her lip.

"Why me? Why not another witch? The Edge is full of us."

It's a fair question. She's anything but stupid.

Thorn sighs. "This bit is complicated, and due to the sensitive nature of the situation and our need for confidentiality, we aren't at liberty to divulge any more information at this time."

His speech couldn't be more scripted. I clear my throat. *I'm the one who is supposed to be in charge now, remember, guys?*

"So what am I supposed to do with this information?" She takes another bite of her cake, leans back, and crosses her arms over her chest.

She's gone into protection mode and I'm not surprised, with all our pussyfooting around the actual subject matter.

"Trust us?" I throw her my most innocent smile, trying to disarm. "We suspect the rogue vampire will come after you. You're the only one who can positively identify him." It's not an outright lie, just a slight omission.

"And—" Dominic starts, then stops when *both* Thorn and Rhys throw him a look. Good to know I'm not the only one uncomfortable with this bullshit."

"What the hell aren't you guys telling me?"

"We're sorry, Iphi, but this is a need-to-know basis," says Thorn, who is glaring openly at Dominic now.

"What *can* you talk about then? You know who the vampire is but you can't tell me. You know why he's in the Edge but you can't tell me. You know why he's interested in me but you can't tell me. Anything else I'm missing? Or can't you tell me?" She piles another bite of cake into her mouth and slams the plate down in front of me.

Our eyes lock and hers soften, almost like she's

giving me silent kudos for being the one not treating her like an imbecile.

The rest of the guys avert their gazes, looking down at their plates, each one focusing extra hard on taking a bite and then passing their plates to the right.

I may as well do the same, and I gulp the last of the upside-down chocolate cake that I assume is Iphigenia's favorite. And I can see why, it's delicious.

Iphi growls low next to me, then lets out a long sigh and leans back. "Look, I get it. You're all trying to protect me."

The woman has the endearing quality of forgiving us for our secrets. *Doesn't hold grudges.* I silently add up all of her pluses and realize I'm going to need a third hand soon.

"We'd like to watch you," says Thorn a minute later.

"Thorn," I admonish and he shrugs.

"Excuse me?" Her mouth is full of food, so it sounds more like, "Scoozey?"

"What Thorn means is that, in order to keep you safe, one of us would like to follow you when you're alone outside," I interject. I give Thorn a warning look, to which he responds by shooting up a middle finger.

"You can't be sure he'll approach me again," she says.

"It's not a matter of if; it's a matter of when."

"Caspian is right," says Rhys. "He *will* come after you. We need to keep an eye out."

"Need to or want to?" Her fingertips twitch around the fork poised in front of her mouth, sugary syrup dripping back onto the plate. "I'm experiencing conflicting emotions about this, guys. I can't tell if it's because you care about my safety or are just keen on vanquishing the monster."

I touch her shoulder. "We all care, Iphigenia, it's no more than that."

But Thorn coughs. Really, Thorn? Now? And her eyes move from mine to his.

Nostrils flaring, she says, "Or maybe I'm bait."

"We would never use an innocent girl to lure a suspected villain. Keeping the peace and protecting the safety of our citizens is our top priority." The rogue vampire already sees her as bait and maybe my brothers do, too, but not me. I see her as a woman who needs our protection, even more so because she incorrectly believes herself to be invincible.

"What if I don't agree?" She plops the last of the fritter into her mouth and gulps it down, practically unchewed.

We all exchange looks. "Why wouldn't you?" asks Thorn.

"For one, because I am not some helpless child. Two, because I like my independence. I already have a helicopter mother. When I'm out of my house, I like to be alone."

Her mouth is open a moment longer, as if to add something else, but she clamps it shut.

"We hadn't anticipated you saying no," Rhys says into the silence.

"Sorry, guys, I don't want to disappoint. Let's revisit this later." She smiles at us, blinking.

"Okay, whatever you need."

She scoots out of the booth and stands up. "This has been a *fun* evening." The emphasis on "fun" sounds anything but. "Have a great night. All of you." She nods to each of us as Rhys shoots to his feet.

"Wait, I'll drive you home."

"No, thanks, I need some alone time." She holds up her hand. "If I get a say in all of this, I'm choosing not to have anyone trail me 'for my own safety.' And I choose to walk home on my own. Unaccompanied." Before anyone can respond, she turns and leaves.

"Great," says Dominic. "That did not go well. Why the hell didn't you guys let me talk? I'm the one with the training. I could have convinced her."

"No manipulation." I shove my long hair behind my ears again. I really need to get it cut.

"But if we tell her who the rogue vampire is, she may not help us, even if it's in her own interest," says Thorn. "We have to look out for her. There's a reason that vampire is here and it's not to make nice."

Rhys holds a hand up. "Stop it. You guys are the law and I get that. I respect that. But he's my responsibility. You forget how well I know him. There's got to be a reason he disappeared without saying anything to me. He's never been evil. There's no way he's acting on his own free will."

"Are you saying you don't want him taken in?" Thorn leaps up, chest rising, his full bulk on display.

"I know what will happen if he is. He won't be given a fair trial. It'll be worse than a banishment."

"We have to find out what the hell is going on. And that little girl is our key."

I stand up, too. Dominic is the only one left in his seat, examining us like we're a group therapy session gone irretrievably wrong. "She's not our pawn, Thorn, and she's not a little girl."

"You have feelings for her? You don't even know her."

"She's a good person. A young *woman* with her entire life ahead of her."

"Which is exactly why she needs our protection," says Dominic. "You can sit and fight about it but I'm going after her." He gets up to leave.

I put my hand on his arm. "Look, you all need to calm down and take a few breaths." I look each one of them in the eye, let them see my resolve. "I'll go. I'll keep her safe. Okay?"

The men grumble but they sit back down.

CHAPTER EIGHT

IPHIGENIA

*W*hat I didn't tell the men was that I really just needed a break from feeling everyone's feelings all the time. Thus, with a confusing mixture of anger, annoyance, and gratitude, I walk through the well-lit center of town. Our town actually has three downtown areas. There's Plum Street, which is where most of the Edgers do their shopping and hang out. There's the town center, where the municipal buildings are gathered. And then there's the boardwalk, of course. Where the tourists gather to gawk at the Signum, even though they can't tell us apart at a glance. That doesn't stop them from making up stories, though, no matter how ignorant or hurtful. They'll go back to their human towns and brag, "I saw vampires, shifters, werewolves, and witches." Oh, my. Though if I weren't a Signum, perhaps I'd feel the same way.

The boardwalk is always lit up at night, even though only a few restaurants like Confections are open. Out-of-towners like to window-shop their way down to the pier and then walk along the boardwalk before they go dancing or drinking. The thoughts and feelings of so many happy tourists usually blur into a cheerful white noise for me, but tonight I can't find my center. I'm too annoyed.

So why am I annoyed with the guys' proposal? It's true that I'm so over being watched by Mother. I can barely tolerate it when I'm home, so the thought of being beholden to yet more babysitters while I'm out and about rubs me raw. I only stay at Mom's because everyone else has left; otherwise, I'd have moved out as well. I have the finances to do it. But I don't want to hurt her like my sisters have. Like my father did.

I leave the brightly lit downtown area behind me and continue along the highway, staring out at the dark ocean. Tonight the moon is a waning crescent, lending darkness and shadows to the already blackened night. I don't even bother to take out my self-defense spray or whistle, so insistent am I that I can take care of myself. I've walked these streets alone, at night, for years with no problems. Even when I was as young as twelve.

I sigh. Now is not the time to let my injured pride injure me in truth. Turning up the side street leading to my house, I rummage in my purse for the spray and noisemaker, but only because the shifter brothers have me a little on edge. Something rustles nearby, and then I'm lying flat on the ground, on my back, the wind knocked out of me, my purse and weapons scattered. The vampire from the night before is straddling me, his putrid breath drowning my senses. Yikes, my amulet didn't work?

He leans closer, sniffing at me, and his eyes snap shut for a moment. "Why aren't you afraid of me?" he hisses, making no move to bite.

He's right. I'm not afraid. I know he won't hurt me. He does nothing to hide his emotions; they're laid out for all who can feel them. Even though I'm not exactly on top of the situation here, I sense that he's only looking for conversation. Sadness and remorse stream off of him. "Because I'm a witch."

"Witch," he hisses, "yes. But what kind of witch?"

I'm tempted to respond with, "Why, Glenda the Good Witch, of course," but I refrain. This is no time for jokes. "Just a regular one."

"No. Oh, no. *He* wouldn't want regular."

He? Who the hell is he talking about, and really,

why aren't I terrified? Everything about him is terrifying, especially the way he looks, those horrific scars zigzagging across his face. Without them, he might have been handsome. Once. In a classical Renaissance kind of way . . .

"So pretty," he murmurs, almost to himself. "Maybe that's why . . ." He trails off, creasing his brows and cocking his head. He sniffs the air like a wild animal, all focused intensity. A howl breaks the wind, sending the vampire scurrying backward, and I scramble to my feet. Out of the darkness, a stray dog prowls between us, facing the vampire. The dog growls low in its throat, showing large, pointed teeth, and gnashes them at the vamp, who turns to flee. My defense spray lies just out of reach, on the ground with my purse. Holding my hands up, I take a step backward as the dog whirls around to face me.

Not a dog. A coyote. Shit.

He . . . *Caspian* whimpers and runs off. It was Caspian. I don't know how exactly, but I know it was him. He followed me anyway? Even after I asked him not to?

I'm flooded with both relief and anger. Obviously, the men are right and I'm a target. Goodbye independence, hello shackles. But if I help them catch the baddie, can I just walk away, dust my hands of the mess? That, too, goes against everything

I stand for. I feel sorry for the vampire. I know with every fiber of my being that he does *not* want to be a baddie. And because he reminds me of a lost puppy, I want to help him, not put him behind bars. It's not his fault he's cursed. Is it? Maybe, like Carter's younger brother, he was cursed for something someone else close to him did. I'll have to talk to the poor vamp to find out, but if he approaches me again, it's likely one of my protectors will intervene.

I walk the rest of the way home, thinking about how I can simultaneously slip past them and keep them in my life. After all, they are four stunning men and they are all interested in me. No, they are only interested in what they *need* from me.

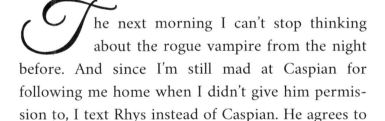

The next morning I can't stop thinking about the rogue vampire from the night before. And since I'm still mad at Caspian for following me home when I didn't give him permission to, I text Rhys instead of Caspian. He agrees to meet me at the Harbor House Cafe for breakfast.

Thirty minutes later, he pulls out a chair for me and I plop down. "I'm glad you asked me to meet you."

"You are?" I blow a curl out of my eye.

"Very much so." He sits across the table. "I was worried we upset you last night at Confections."

"You did, a little," I admit.

"That wasn't the intention. You know that, right?"

"I do." I chew on my lip. "But you guys were right; I am a target."

Rhys leans toward me, pressing his elbows to the table. "What happened?"

I almost lose my concentration; he sure has that whole Ren angel look down, as though he's employed the sun to permanently cast a golden beam of light to shine down on him. "He made an appearance last night. But surely you already know that, since Caspian intervened." I lean back and cross my arms. We pause when the waiter appears and pours us coffee.

"Look. We all understand that you want to be independent and we want that for you, too. But in order for that to happen, you may need our help in the interim."

I pour cream into my coffee but instead of sipping it, I swirl it endlessly with a spoon. "Why? That's my question."

"Why do you need our help?" Rhys reaches for his coffee.

"Why do you want to protect me? Is it because you need me?"

He shakes his head, slowly, then takes a sip of the warm liquid. "We want to help you because we care about you."

"But you hardly know me."

Rhys licks his lips. "We know enough."

I cock my head. "What's that mean?"

"I saw Aurelia hovering at the door the other night when I picked you up. You told us at Confections how much you hate that. So why on earth do you put up with it? You keep fighting us for your independence, insisting on taking care of yourself, yet you let your mother walk all over you?" His tone is light, questioning, not accusing.

"It's complicated. I know how much my mother has lost, how much of her own life she's given up for us. For me. How my sisters don't really understand her motivations. But I do and it's my responsibility to . . ."

"What?" Rhys leans forward and places his hand on mine. "Your mother is not your responsibility, Iphi. She's a grown woman who's made her choices and gets to take care of herself. She's the mother, not you."

I look at his hand over mine on the table. I tap

my nails underneath it but he traces calming circles over the top and I stop.

"You're one of the kindest people any of us has ever met. You care about everyone around you, often putting them before yourself in detriment to yourself. I can't imagine anyone knowing you and not wanting to help you or take care of you."

Though his last words rub me the wrong way—I don't want to be "taken care of"—I appreciate the sentiment. My instinct is to snap at him, but I bite my tongue. Rhys is genuinely concerned and trying to look out for me. His cousins, I'm not so sure about. "Can you tell me why the rogue vampire is interested in me and who he is?"

Rhys's eyes shift away. "I can't."

"Can't or won't?"

"Look, Iphigenia, what matters here is your safety. We don't want him near you again."

"Are you going to kill him?"

His chair slides back. "No, of course not. That's not an option."

I let out a relieved sigh.

"Can I ask you a question?"

"Of course."

"Are you happy?"

I haven't really asked myself this question before. I consider myself a positive, carefree person, though

I don't ever give the h-word much thought. "I have things in my life that make me happy, like the circus."

He smiles but it doesn't reach his eyes. "That's not what I'm talking about."

"What then?"

"This is just an observation, not a judgment."

I nod.

"Well . . . all of your friends and your sisters, even your mother, are living their lives."

"And I'm not?"

"I don't think so. From where I stand, it looks like you're living for those around you."

I take a sip of my coffee, then place it back on the table. "I don't really get what you mean. How am I living for someone else?"

He leans back in his chair, pushing his dark hair out of his eyes. "Why do you *really* still live with your mother?"

I close my eyes for a moment. When I open them he hasn't moved. "I stay with Mom because she needs me."

Rhys's head shakes from side to side, his eyes trained on mine. "There's another reason, Iphigenia. One that's all your own and has nothing to do with Aurelia."

"I don't know what you mean."

"I don't want to overstep any boundaries or make you feel uncomfortable."

"No," I wave my hand in the air, "go on. I'd rather know what you think."

"There's a part of you that thrives on being needed. Whether Aurelia needs you or not, and I assure you that she doesn't, you stay partly because you're getting *your* needs met. Who would you be without your mother?"

If I weren't an empath, his words would sting. I fight back the intense heat flooding my system and focus instead on his emotions. What I pick up is concern for my well-being, deep caring, and something like . . . love? That can't be right. The sensation makes me reel more than his words do.

"I understand that you're concerned, I really do, but I don't agree with your assessment. I'm confident in who I am, I'm present in my body, and I have a fantastic career. I don't *need* my mother. It's just that everyone else left her. It's my duty to stay so she doesn't keep getting hurt."

He takes another sip of his coffee, letting his eyes do all the talking. They say, *You're fooling yourself Iphigenia, not me*. Stupid empathy. Sure, my life's not perfect but no one's is. Do I love living with my mother? No, but I don't hate it either. She makes it easy for me. I don't have to cook, Alistair is a doll, and Mother is always eager to help me with spell casting.

"Oh, darling, look who's here," a sultry voice purrs next to my ear. I turn, smiling at Burgundy and her girlfriend, Tiyah, both beaming down at me.

"Ladies." Rhys rises, kissing them both on the cheek and I flush with jealousy.

Really, Iphi? What the hell?

"It's wonderful to see you both," Tiyah says. "We just wanted to say hello, but we won't intrude on your breakfast." She pulls Burgundy toward a table already occupied by their third, Elijah, who waves at us and then stands to pull out the chairs for his ladies.

Before they sit, though, Burg wraps her arms around her girlfriend's thin frame and pulls her in for a hot kiss, then Elijah. In public. Without a care in the world. She doesn't care at all what other people think. The three of them look like they just stepped out of the pages of *Vogue* together.

Wow. Here's their relationship out in the open, yet the crowd at the Harbor House has already lost interest and is moving on with their morning. I peek left and right but no one's staring.

"Well," Rhys says, snapping my attention back to him. "If you want to move, or even if you're looking for a little break, we have plenty of room on our property. You could even have your own little house."

I shift uncomfortably in my seat. "Oh, thank you for the offer but I don't need a place to stay." I blow my hair out of my face. "I'm perfectly happy living at home, with Mom."

He bites his lip, one of his fangs momentarily snagging the dark flesh.

"Really. It's fine. Aurelia doesn't treat me the same way she treats other people or even my sisters. We have a really good relationship, an understanding."

He nods, but his thoughts prickle with something like fear. *That's only because you haven't done anything she doesn't agree with. Yet.*

Ignoring him, I glance back at the thruple. A fresh plate of food sits in front of each of them. Tiyah is picking off of Burgundy's plate and Burg swats her hand away playfully. Elijah picks off of Burgundy's plate, too, just like Tiyah did, and every few bites he places a bite in each of their mouths with his hands, fork be damned. They joke and exchange words, their interactions effortless, like the petals of a flower blowing in the wind. Connected and strong even when challenged.

It's the most romantic and sensual thing I've ever seen.

I've never had that or anything like it. No one to pick food off my plate or kiss me in public.

"Do you like that?" Rhys growls in my ear and I color quickly, picking up my coffee to hide my obvious discomfort. "They're a beautiful triad, don't you agree?"

"Yes, of course." I don't look up at him, suddenly engrossed in my water cup.

"I don't mean physically, I mean the way they interact. Their relationship is smooth, seamless. They make it seem easy."

"Yeah," I agree, "I don't understand how they do it. The three of them look and act as if they've been part of one another's lives for eighty years instead of eight months."

"I think that's the way it works when everything clicks into place."

"Have you ever had that?" I jut my chin toward their table.

"Never. You?"

I shake my head, not wanting to tell him that, in love, I'm almost as inexperienced as one can get.

CHAPTER NINE

IPHIGENIA

*R*hys insists on driving me home even though it's early and a beautiful day to walk.

"Can you park at the end of the drive, behind the oak tree so . . . ?"

"Of course," he says without asking me to clarify. He knows.

"I really appreciate the ride," I say as he pulls over.

He stops the car and leans toward me, so close his intoxicating scent fills my nostrils. "Do you have any plans for tonight?"

I shake my head because my mouth is so dry I couldn't speak even if I wanted to.

"Come dancing with me."

Oh, how I want to say yes. "At the V? Nah. It's not my cup of tea. Plus, it's twenty-one and over."

"Not the V, at Promise." He leans even closer, our noses almost touching. I close my eyes, expecting a kiss, torn between wanting one and not wanting one. After a second, the air cools in front of me and I open my eyes. He's leaning back in his seat.

I turn my head and look out the window. "I don't really dance." A shadow flashes between the sun and the car.

"You don't dance? What? You're kidding, right? With the grace of your aerial and contortion acts? Surely you move like a professional on the dance floor."

"No, I don't dance."

"'Don't' meaning you don't like to?"

I chew on my lower lip. A painful past I've kept to myself, forever. Like a dirty little secret. Isn't there a saying about shining a light on something? Maybe by bringing it out into the open, the pain will dissipate. Rhys looks at me expectantly but he doesn't say anything. He's open to whatever I have to say, without judgment. And because he's hiding a deep wound of his own, I know he's the one I can tell. If I don't open up now, I may never get past this.

I pull in a deep breath and clutch the seat on

either side of me as though I'm on a roller coaster, teetering at the top before the long drop down.

"When I was in middle school—" I stop and he puts his hand over mine, urging me to continue. "I had an innocent crush on this guy." He rubs the back of my hand, methodically, back and forth. "I went to the school dance, just hoping to see him, and was ecstatic when he pulled me out on the dance floor."

My smile could have lit up the entire room that night, waves of triumph and confidence burning through my body. Nothing mattered in that moment but him and me dancing together, and I completely let go, enjoying myself more in that singular, tiny space of time than I ever had before.

"But there was this other girl there, mocking me behind my back." I remember bringing my eyes up to my crush's, expecting his smile to mirror mine, but he was laughing at something behind me. I spun around and there was this mean girl, Justine Miller, aping me, exaggerating every movement with jerky, flopping limbs out of synch with the music. "I cried and ran off the dance floor and, well, there you have it, scarred for life. I never danced again."

"So she transferred her own glaring insecurities onto you?" Rhys peels my hand from the upholstery and clutches it tightly. "Like a game of cooties."

"I know it doesn't really make sense. I know she

only did it because she was jealous of me and trying to steal my power. But . . ."

"It worked. And you've let it keep you from dancing for how long?"

I count on my fingers and laugh. "More years than I'd like to admit."

Rhys turns and looks out of his car window, then back to me, sighing. "Thank you for sharing that with me."

My cheeks flush and I peek at him through my lashes.

"I had some challenges growing up as well and I just want you to know that now four mighty men have your back."

I nod and my cheeks stretch into a wide grin. "Thank you, that means a lot."

"Tonight then? I'll pick you up at ten." He leans over and places a firm, closemouthed kiss on my cheek.

Exiting the car, I wonder how I'll get past Aurelia later. Lie? I hate doing that and I'm not very good at it. Omit? I could pretend to go to bed early and sneak out. In all my twenty years, I've been the good girl, the role Sadie refused to play and Chrys rebelled against at twenty-five.

Placing my key in the lock, I wait for the familiar click. Aurelia has insisted on making our locks magical so no one can pick them, something that happened for a short time in other parts of town. I think she's being paranoid, but she's racked up a lot more time on this earth than I have, so I don't question it.

"Darling." She's hovering just beyond the entrance. How does she always know when I'm coming home? The brand she put on the back of my neck is essentially a magical GPS for emergencies, but surely she has better things to do than spy on me with her crystal ball. "Did you and Burgundy have a nice breakfast?"

"We did, thank you." I avert my gaze quickly. Sometimes she knows when I'm lying and this one I need to cover up. "Did you and Al enjoy your morning?"

"We did," she responds stiffly. "Darling, aren't you spending an awful lot of time with Burgundy?" She reaches out to tuck a curl behind my ear.

"I guess. Why?"

"Well, dearest." She tries to flatten my curls, which I hate. The more someone touches my hair, the frizzier it becomes and I shake my head to dislodge her prying fingers. "She's not the best influence."

"What do you mean?"

"She's a stripper and a home-wrecker."

I bristle at her judgmental, ignorant label. My mother knows me well enough to know I would never agree. "So?"

"It's just that you're not like that."

"Like what? I'm not a stripper and I'm not in a *triad*?" Thanks for pointing out the obvious, Mom.

She lifts up another strand of my hair, shifting it from my shoulder to my back. "You don't have loose morals." My mother's multicolored eyes pin me in place.

I hold my hand up. "First of all, Mother, I don't think that Burgundy has loose morals either. She's happy in her relationship, and so are Elijah and Tiyah. And second, who cares if she does? She's a good person who treats me with respect."

"I just don't think—"

I turn and head toward my room.

"Do not walk away from me when I'm talking to you, young lady," she hisses.

"What's this?" Alistair approaches from the other end of the hallway. His welcoming grin disappears as I stomp past him without a word.

"She's impossible." Mother doesn't bother lowering her voice. "Just like her sisters."

I slam my door behind me, just like Sadie used to. I never understood why she did that. Until now. Why does Aurelia have to judge everyone else like that? It's not like there's a one size fits all with life. Everyone gets to make their own decisions, and what's right for one person isn't necessarily right for another. I understand that—I *feel* that—and give everyone room to be themselves. Even my mother. Especially her. It is, however, becoming clear that she does not return the favor.

⚬ ◆ ✖ ◆ ⚬

J decide not to tell Aurelia that I'm meeting Rhys at Promise later. She'd probably lock me in my room and spell the windows shut if she knew. Instead, I pretend I'm tired and turn into bed early. It's a little sad how good I've become at this act, and I arouse no suspicion.

Once I'm tucked neatly inside, I light four white candles and place them around my room, one for each cardinal direction. I remove my athame from a dresser drawer and use it to invoke pentacles in the air while reciting incantations at each compass point. When the circle is cast—with me, a casting candle, my herbs and my crystal ball in the center—I start weaving my spells.

The first one I choose is a door-locking spell. Mother has never allowed any of us to have locks and I've never minded much in the past. I didn't have anything to hide, though my sisters certainly did. But now I wonder what privacy would feel like, and even though I'm allowed to cast spells on my own, I don't want her barging in and asking me about them.

I don't have my own grimoire, but I do know how to cast minor spells without looking them up. Maybe I can improvise a little, cast something more than minor.

I add a pinch of clove and a walnut leaf to the burning candle. *"Claude ostium."* *Close the door* in Latin.

Sadie spent the last year taking classes at our local college on spell casting and Latin. I used to be the one who showed her the arts, since Mother kept her ignorant of so much magic, but now that she's grown into her power, she's the one teaching both me and Chrys whenever she can. I'm not fluent in Latin yet like Sadie is, but I am a quick study.

I recite the phrase two more times and throw my hands out toward the door handle. I hope that it's working but I can't test it without breaking the circle. Maybe Mom will stay away and not put it to the test.

I focus on my next spell. To sneak out later and make it look like I'm still in bed, I need to cast a spell of mixed perception. Aurelia taught me how to cast this particular spell years ago when she was spying on Chrys.

A pinch of cinnamon, two of chicory, and one of aconite. The flame licks my hand, and I pull back with a yelp, then cast my eyes toward the door, expecting Mother to burst through any second. A minute later, I relax and recite the next spell on a long stream of breath. *"Videbunt oculi insar est falsum in lectulo."* *Eyes see a false likeness in my bed.*

Next, I sit down on my wood floor, cradling my crystal ball in my lap. Passing my left hand over the top, I ask, "Where is the rogue vampire now?" The crystal churns inside like smoke billowing up from a raucous campfire. When it clears I squeal, the ball sliding off my lap and rolling heavily across the floor.

"Iphigenia?" Mother's voice calls out on the other side of my door, followed by frantic knocking. Aurelia, knocking? That's a first.

"I'm fine, Mom. Please don't come in."

The handle turns. My eyes dart wildly around the room, not sure what to clean up first, but the door holds.

"Why is your door locked?" she says through clenched teeth. "Unlock it this instant."

"It must be stuck." I blow out the candles and scoop everything under my bed. "One sec."

The door continues to rattle, Mother twisting and turning the handle. I'm on my feet and jumping toward the door when it's flung open, her reddish hair flying around her head as if caught in a heavy wind. The look in her eyes is crazed, her nostrils expanded, lips pursed. "What. Is. Going. On?"

"Nothing." I flash her a toothy, innocent smile but she just wags a finger at me.

"If I find out you've been up to no good, Iphigenia—"

"Me?"

"I will kick you out of this house so fast—"

"Mama." I hold my hands up in what I hope is a placating gesture. "You know I could move out anytime I want to. I'm the one who's chosen to remain here. With you."

She scents the air, ignoring my plea. "What were you burning?"

"I lit a candle." I motion toward one of the four, still on my vanity. The others are safely scattered under my bed.

"A white candle? A *ritual* white candle?"

"Is it?" I cross over and wrap my hand around it, bringing it up to eye level. "Oh, you're right. Silly me."

Mother huffs but thankfully turns to go. Before exiting, she opens and closes my bedroom door several times and then eyes me over her shoulder. "Keep your bedroom door open until you go to sleep tonight."

"Sure thing, Mom."

It's unusual for me but I can't tune out my thoughts, which tumble mercilessly down the shores of Aurelia. Rhys seems to have set this all in motion with his comments.

My love for my mother is fierce but the way she treats me is taking its toll, wearing me down like a piece of glass caught in the shallows of a churning current for years on end. My surfaces, too, are flat, the rough edges polished away, fine cracks smoothed out. What, then, makes that piece of rock different from any other piece? Do I even have my own personality? Am I an individual or am I merely the person my mother wants me to be?

Smooth, without flaw, featureless.

Bland.

CHAPTER TEN

CASPIAN

"*I* need to talk to you," Rhys says.

"Sure. Sure." It's been a long day at work and I'm feeling every sleepless hour of last night, but the intent look on Rhys's face wakes me up a little. I take a step toward the back of the station, figuring we can talk in the interview room for privacy, but he holds up a hand.

"Not inside. Grab the others and meet me outside in five."

It must be important. Rhys isn't one to demand anything. I text the others and walk out to the front of the station where he's waiting on one of the benches.

"What's up?" I ask.

He holds up a finger and we sit in silence until the others join us. "I have been with Iphi all morning," he starts and we exchange glances. "First, I wanted you all to know that I'm developing feelings for her and I think she's developing them for me too."

Shit, I'm too late? I want to scream at him and tell him that I have feelings for her, too. I suspect we all may be interested in the Flying Seraphim but are either too polite or too hardheaded to say anything. Well, probably not Dom, he doesn't seem to even like her as a person, let alone romantically. I want to be happy for Rhys but in the moment, envy takes over. I swallow back a growl. Dominic shoots me a look, his eyebrows raised.

"But that doesn't mean she's not interested in one of you as well." He's looking at me. So much for trying not to broadcast my own interest.

"Really, man?" says Thorn. "So you and Caspian are going to fight over some hot piece of ass?"

"Hey." Dominic steps in front of Thorn. "That's incredibly misogynistic and Rhys doesn't sound like he's interested in fighting any of us for anything. Surely you know him better than that."

Thorn huffs. "Right, of course. I forgot, him and Caspian share *everything.*"

"Stop it," Rhys snaps. "Nothing's happening on that front right this second. I just wanted you to know what's going on with me. More importantly, we all know my brother is after her but she doesn't seem afraid."

"No, she doesn't." I rub my hands together. "She almost looked annoyed with me last night when I intervened."

"What the hell does Nolan want with her?" asks Dominic.

"I'm not sure." Rhys runs his hands through his hair. " We know he came here for her. He may have been told to find her. Whoever is pulling his strings may have a personal interest in her. Or maybe it's as simple as him believing she can help him beat this because she's a witch from the strongest family in the Edge."

"And if he did any research on her," I add, "he'd know she has a bleeding heart for the downtrodden as well."

"That does make her an easy mark," grumbles Thorn.

"More importantly," says Dominic, "maybe she *can* help him. Maybe the others, too."

"What the hell does it matter?" Thorn's voice rises. "He needs to be stopped. And nothing can help the ghouls. All we can do is put them down."

"You act like you don't have a heart, but you're not fooling any of us."

Thorn narrows his eyes at Dominic, jaw clenched, but he doesn't respond.

"Does she understand the danger he poses? Has she seen any signs of the ghouls yet?" I ask.

"I don't think so," Rhys sighs. "She might not recognize them if she did, though. We would recognize one on sight, even if it hadn't fully devolved yet. She doesn't want us following her, but one of you, in your shifts, is going to anyway. Understood?"

I nod and look at Dominic, who shrugs and looks at Thorn. Why does Dom always have to put on such a front? Is he lying to us or to himself, acting like he doesn't care about the girl? Thorn, on the other hand, nods without a moment's hesitation, though ordinarily he'd bristle at being dictated to.

Thorn is the oldest, our pack leader, and the only father figure we had for much of our lives. He's built a solid front of nothing-to-see-here, but he's also the one who remembers our parents the most, lived with them the longest. He's the one who was hit the hardest when we lost them and our home. As the youngest, I had my older brothers to care for me and was more malleable than the others. Dominic's way of dealing with it was to study psychology, while Rhys used his fists. Nolan drifted farther and farther from us before he eventually cut us out altogether. So the burden always fell on Thorn, our protector.

He's afraid to let himself fall in love. It's easier for him to jump in and save people than send them on their way before they can ditch him.

And as though he can read my thoughts, he speaks up. "I'll help with the Iphi situation, but only because she's Nolan bait and I want that situation fixed."

"Fine," I say. "As long as you're on board, the why doesn't matter."

"We need a plan," says Dominic. "Something solid that can use Iphigenia to help us capture Nolan."

I shift uncomfortably. "How can we protect her while using her as bait?"

Dominic sighs. "There are four of us. We can protect her. We're strong, and we all have powers. She won't be in danger." He offers Rhys a tight smile.

"He's right," Thorn huffs, "we're a force to be reckoned with and I'm itching for a fight." He punches his own hand.

I roll my eyes. I'm surrounded by testosterone-poisoned idiots.

"That doesn't sound like much of a plan, Dominic, but we don't have a lot of leeway right now," says Rhys.

Thorn stops pacing. "She won't get hurt. She's got us, and she's got that protection medallion thingy, right?"

Rhys nods. "I'm meeting her tonight at Promise. It would be best if we're all there. I want her to get used to being around all of us together. That way it won't be so obvious that we're her personal bodyguards."

I can get behind that. Shit, I'd like to get behind *her*. From the eager look on some of my brothers' faces, I'm not the only one.

CHAPTER ELEVEN

IPHIGENIA

*W*aiting until ten o'clock in order to sneak out of the house proves more difficult than I anticipated. My heart races uncomfortably and I take another shower after I drench myself in nervous sweat. Texting Burgundy, I ask her to be my wingwoman at the dance club, and she agrees. Getting a ride from her will cut down on my jitters, and she consents to meeting me a couple of blocks over.

I feign exhaustion after dinner and escape to my room, setting up the fake Iphi illusion in my bed.

It takes me close to an hour to get ready, more to kill time than out of vanity. And because I have to keep my mind off the fact that I'm going dancing tonight. Sitting in front of my mirror, I gather my locks, pinning each one up carefully so they form a bright halo around my head. The curls cascade down in soft waves, reminiscent of a mermaid underwater. Refusing to wear foundation, I make up my eyes with a natural-looking-blush eye shadow and light-brown mascara. Then I line my lips in pink and fill in my plump bottom lip and the Cupid's bow on my top lip with a shiny mauve.

The night air is warm in June, and I choose a sundress. It's black with a base of tiny flowers and it buttons up the bodice. I grab a purple sweater in case it gets cooler and my favorite pair of silver strappy heels. I've trained myself to wear heels as a performer, but also because I'm just not that tall.

Climbing out of my window proves easy enough, after I remove the screen and stash it in my closet. Mother has phenomenal hearing so I tiptoe around barefoot, dropping my sweater, purse, and shoes out of the window into the bushes, where each lands with a small thud.

Footsteps down the hallway toward my room freeze me in place. There's a soft rap on my door before it opens a crack. Oh no, I forgot to re-do the door locking spell. My heart jumps into my throat, beating so loudly that I'm sure Burgundy can hear it two streets over, where she's sitting in her car, waiting for me.

Light pours in from the hallway as Mother

cranes her head inside. "Iphi?" she calls softly. I stand completely still in front of the window, holding my breath, and praying to the Moon Goddess and Pan and any other deity I can think of that my spell will work. The door doesn't open further, but Mother stays poised there for a moment, sniffing the air. Crap, the window is open.

"Is everything all right, darling?" Alistair says from behind her.

"Yes, dear. Don't talk too loudly, she's asleep." Her head disappears and the door closes with a soft snick.

The breath I let out is far too noisy, but the illusion spell worked and I want to do a little dance. Instead, I call out a thank-you to the moon and Pan and hoist myself out the window.

Landing with a thud, I dust myself off, then gather my purse and don my sweater and shoes. There's a faint curdled-milk scent on the wind that prickles the hairs on my arm, but I tell myself it's nothing and walk down our lane toward Burgundy's car.

As I turn onto the next block, the rancid smell wafts by again, stronger this time. My head darts left, then right, but nothing is there. A twig snaps. The trees overhead rustle in the breeze. One more step and the monster vampire lands in front of me with a thud as though dropped from above.

Shouting with surprise, I hold my hands up, palms out, and take a step backward.

"Iphigenia." My name sounds like the wind coursing through the sails of a phantom pirate ship. "Please . . ."

His eyes are the darkest of blacks, as if they're nothing but two large pupils. He has no iris and no sclera. This, more than his scars and savage teeth, scares the bejesus out of me.

"Don't hurt me," I finish, breathless.

He takes a step backward, shaking his long, dark, ratted hair. "Never hurt you. Looking for you."

"Me? Why?"

The rogue vampire looks at the ground in front of him. I follow his gaze, noticing for the first time how shattered he is. It's more than his tattered clothing, which is nothing more than strips and holes. More than the crazy look in those blackened eyes. More than the stench wafting off him, so pungent I have to clench my mouth shut and swallow repeatedly to keep from heaving.

He raises his gaze and tilts his head, the movements short and jerky, almost robotic. His head doesn't swivel on his neck, it cranes unnaturally. "Your heart," he finally says.

Instinctively, I clutch both of my hands to my chest. "You want my *heart*?" I practically scream, backing away.

"No," now he's the one holding up his palms, "not like that."

"What then?" I keep backing up.

"No one's spoken to me in so long."

"What happened to you? Who *are* you?"

"My name is monster. No, Nolan. No, monster. Made so by another's hands." He snorts. "That's what keeps me going day after day. Who I want to be . . ."

My senses practically scream his sincerity, though his words are all but unintelligible. The idea of starting over fresh each new day, hoping to reinvent himself—the sensation pouring off Nolan is almost tangible. Yesterday is gone and tomorrow has yet to come, but today . . . is a blank slate. "Where do I fit into that?"

"Master wants you for himself."

"What!" I shriek.

"But I won't let him hurt you. Ever."

"Have you been following me to kidnap me?"

"I don't want to. I fight not to. You glow so brightly, a beacon. A reminder of what I've lost. Goodness here, in the world. I will protect you."

"I . . . glow?"

"It's how I follow you. All the others, too. The ones I made. You glow, a bright light in the night."

I have no idea what he's talking about. Was this a spell cast upon me so he'd always be able to locate me? "Why do the shifters and my vampire friend want you, too?" I ask. "To help you?"

His ragged form shakes. Though he drank just the other night, he looks like he hasn't had sustenance for months. "I don't know. I fear not."

"What do you think they want from you?"

"They must seek my master, the ever-changing one. The nightmare. For me, destruction."

I hope not. Killing is not something I can condone. "What would they want with your master?"

"To defeat him."

I shake my head, inhale deeply, and hold it, trying to focus on the face in front of me. Trying to parse why he looks so familiar.

"Iphigenia," he takes a step toward me, "I'm so hungry. I'm starving all the time."

I take a step away but my back hits a tree.

His head jerks and tilts, the angle oddly insectile. When he blinks, the blackened orbs snap like a camera lens. In an instant, the pupils split vertically, like the eyes of a cat, before blinking back to utter blackness.

When he lunges for me, I'm unprepared. One minute, we're having a civil conversation and the next . . .

His hands grasp the air in front of my body, clutching at nothing. Fingers open and close a few inches from my nose. An invisible barrier separates us. My amulet. At least it's working now. Maybe it only protects me when someone intentionally wants to physically harm me?

"You think you can evade me, girl?" The voice that comes from Nolan's mouth is not his, not anymore, but there's something eerily familiar about it.

My sisters, my mother, the guys, *anyone* would label me naive, but I know in my bones that Nolan would never hurt me. But the thing that stands in front of me now is not the rogue vampire. It's his puppet master.

"Release Nolan," I command, head held high, shoulders squared.

"In exchange for you? Gladly. Give yourself to me, *Iphigenia*." The way he hisses my name claws all the air out of my lungs. Like I'm a drowning rat in a sea of rats, listening to the sounds of their shrieks, my own shrieks, in the darkness. The sound of claws scraping along a metal wall, scrabbling for purchase. The terrified hisses and writhing bodies flailing against one another, the weak used as life rafts.

"How do I know y-you?" So much for sounding brave.

Nolan's hands grasp at my face, not quite connecting. My amulet is keeping him at bay but he's still far too close for comfort.

A growl snaps me out of my vision, both my head and Nolan's spinning at once. A yard away is a lion, teeth gnashing, saliva glistening in the moonlight. The beast leaps, knocking Nolan to the ground. The lion perches on top of him, its gaping maw ready to rip out Nolan's throat.

"Wait!" I throw myself on top of the lion without thinking. It—*he* easily knocks me off, but I tumble into a crouch, muscle memory righting me before I even realize what I'm doing. The lion turns his massive head toward me and growls low in his throat. A warning.

Standing tall, I approach the beast. "Do *not* hurt him."

The lion falters at my command. It's one of my cops. Following me again? He roars at me, those long canines sharp and deadly. Nolan scrambles to his feet and runs off. Good.

Mr. Lion stalks toward me, tossing his thick mane, and whipping his tail. I approach, fearless, and he lets me, eyes the color of a sunset trained on me, his majestic form radiating strength, beauty, and violence. Why, then, am I not afraid?

I reach a hand out, and he stands statue-still, awaiting my touch. I hold my hand under his nose but instead of sniffing it, he turns and rubs his head against it. Scratching behind his ear, I want to be mad and yell at him but his fur is so soft and my nose pricks with the scents of lavender and fresh rain. Caspian. This must be his large shift. The scent is intoxicating and I fist his fur and bury my nose in his mane.

A woman's loud shriek breaks the moment.

"*O*h my god, no, girl! Don't move, I'll get a gun." A door away, a neighbor I vaguely recognize turns and flees back inside her house. Humans. You'd think they'd pay closer attention in their orientation meetings.

"Run, Caspian, I'll be fine. Burgundy is waiting for me on the next block. I'll text her and have her pick me up." I hold up my phone and quickly fire one off.

But he tosses his mane at me and stays put.

"If you get shot because of me, how will you

protect me? At least hide from the nosy neighbor, will you? We can talk later about a less noticeable shift. Please?"

Caspian licks my hand, his huge tongue rough but gentle, and pads slowly away until he's out of sight. A moment later, the nosy neighbor returns, holding a shotgun.

"Nothing to see here, ma'am," I say, but she stalks closer.

Her eyes are red rimmed and shifty. She's having a difficult time holding them still and focusing on anything. The shotgun is propped tightly under her arm, her finger on the trigger. Her hands are clenched so tight around it that her knuckles bleed white.

She may accidentally shoot me, or herself. Now is not the time to remind her that guns are illegal in the Edge. If I were Sadie or my mother, I could cast a spell without a ritual. Even Chrys can do it when she gets mad enough. But not me. I'm a powerful witch but only within the confines of a ritual, which in my case usually calls for a drawn circle, fire, and herbs.

At least my amulet will physically protect me. Even if this fool squeezes the trigger, it'll miss. I remind myself to report her weapon to Sheldon though; I do not want a trigger-happy human who doesn't understand gun safety as a neighbor.

"Where is that lion?"

"Ma'am, are you okay?"

Her eyes narrow on me, then widen, and she takes a step closer. Oh, no. It's the same woman Nolan attacked the other night. I didn't recognize her at first because she looks so sickly. Her face is gaunt, her skin hanging off her frame as though she's lost a massive amount of weight. Her dark hair is limp and unwashed. But those eyes . . .

Those are the eyes of a hungry vampire.

Not possible, I assure myself. Vampires are born, not made. That's an old yarn humans spun to scare their children. Her sunken red eyes fix on me and before I can scream, she's in front of me, gnashing her . . . fangs? Again my amulet keeps her from even touching me, but her grinding maw is inches from my face. A bad evening indeed.

With the speed of a vampire, Caspian zooms in and shoves her away from me. Her shotgun goes off and he yelps.

"Caspian!" I lunge for him but he retreats into the bushes. The world grows silent as time moves in slow motion.

"Iphigenia?" Burgundy's voice pierces the air, righting time.

"Burg?" I whirl toward her voice but she's already on top of the neighbor, pinning her against a tree.

"*Redire domum protinus momoria factum est,*" I spit out in utter panic, waving my hand in front of the neighbor's face and then backing away.

Nothing happens. The woman writhes and hisses under Burgundy and I'm about to run for help when my vampire friend sinks her teeth into the woman, dispersing one of the many hormone cocktails at her disposal, no doubt.

Burg releases the woman, who turns as though in a trance and returns to her house, closing the door behind her.

"What was that?" Burg asks, looking around. "Why would a vampire attack you? And was the lion one of your men?"

I nod. "The lion was Caspian. But the vampire, she was turned by the rogue that I told you about. I need to find out if Caspian was shot."

"What do you mean, 'turned'? Let's get to my car, you can call from there. And *explain.*"

"Thank you." My voice is shaky, just like me. I climb into the passenger seat of Cherry, Burgundy's red 1976 Camaro, and try to relax back into the buttery black leather seat, but my entire body is trembling.

"What are you thanking me for?" She glances at me and starts the car.

"For agreeing to this, for being here on time, for saving my life."

"Hey," she pats my shoulder, "you didn't need saving, your amulet would have prevented any harm —or your shifter. Without me, you just would have been treed for a while." She flashes me a fanged smile and my body relaxes a bit.

Burgundy starts the car and I call Rhys.

"Iphi," he greets me warmly. "Don't tell me you're backing out of our dance."

"I'm not, but Caspian may have been shot while in his lion shift. Have you heard anything?"

"No." His voice is all edge now. "Let me call around and get back to you." He hangs up.

"Hey." Burgundy's voice is soft. "This may not help a lot but if he was dead or hurt badly, he wouldn't have been able to run away. Rhys is a vampire and you know we have healing enzymes. He'll fix Caspian up."

"You're right, I'll try not to worry." Easier said than done. I blame myself. If he hadn't been trying to save me, he wouldn't have gotten hurt.

"After you find out he's fine, promise me that you'll either call Sheldon yourself or make sure one of your men files a report for you."

I nod, biting the inside of my cheek.

She puts her hand on my shoulder. "You're

shaken up. You want just a tiny little dose of my feel-good hormones?"

I smirk. "Oxytocin? No thanks, deep breathing is better for me." I take in some air, holding it in my lungs for a beat before letting it out slowly.

"This is probably the wrong time and overstating the obvious but try to enjoy yourself tonight. You've done so much for everyone else, your entire life, me included. This is your time. And you deserve it."

"What have I ever done for you?" I watch the scenery fly by out the window, lulled by the tranquility of the dark water.

"You listened to my family drama and helped sort out the mess I made with Elijah and Tiyah. You listened without judgment, more than anyone else did. The least I can do is give back."

I did listen when she was hurting, but that's what friends are supposed to do. Of course, she didn't know that I could feel her pain as though it were my own. I hold the space people need to lament and offer my ear and solace without judgment. Isn't that what every decent person should do? Simple consideration for others as opposed to putting oneself first.

As the car speeds down the highway, I loll my head out the window like a dog, tasting the wind on my tongue, no longer caring about mussed curls.

There are much more important things in life. Like Caspian's well-being.

My phone pings with a text from Rhys. *Caspian will be fine, not to worry. The rest of us will be a little late to Promise, but we'll be there. Wait for us?*

I let out a long breath, and for the first time since I got into the car, my body slumps back in the seat.

"Good news?" Burgundy asks.

"Caspian's going to be okay."

"No more worrying then." She throws me a smile. "Now it's your time."

"My time?"

"Yeah. Tonight is your time for exploration and fun!"

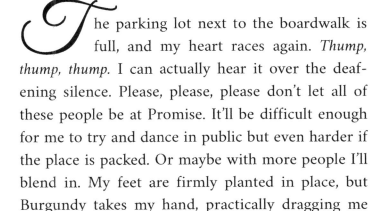

The parking lot next to the boardwalk is full, and my heart races again. *Thump, thump, thump.* I can actually hear it over the deafening silence. Please, please, please don't let all of these people be at Promise. It'll be difficult enough for me to try and dance in public but even harder if the place is packed. Or maybe with more people I'll blend in. My feet are firmly planted in place, but Burgundy takes my hand, practically dragging me down the pier.

"This is not a death sentence." Her laughter sails along the warm summer breeze. "I *promise* you'll have fun at Promise."

I snort and follow her inside the dimly lit structure. I've never been inside the dance club before but I've heard a lot about it. And yet the picture in my mind is nothing like the actual scene. We deposit our shoes by the door and I find myself disappointed that I can't dance in them, or at least wear them to gain a few inches.

The dance floor is full of people, all moving about in different ways. There's a DJ at a table to the left, at the far end of the room. Immediately inside the door, after the shoe repository, people are sitting or stretching atop blue gym mats. Some are even doing yoga. Okay, I can get into that. On the far end of the dance floor, directly across from the entrance, is a raised stage with people lying about or sitting and talking. There's a light show on the far wall that mesmerizes me.

Burg taps my shoulder and points up to the ceiling. Following her hand, my head falling back on my neck, I'm amazed to see another light show overhead. It's almost dizzying, the techno beats and the lights. The swirling dancers in yoga pants and bra tops. She grabs my hand and leads me into the crowd. There's no time for fear or trepidation. If I were to pick the perfect place to let myself go without the dread of possible judgment, this would be it.

"Follow me," she says into my ear and takes both of my hands in hers.

We whirl around in a circle together for so long that I throw my head back and laugh, but it's swallowed up in the seething crowd. Burgundy transfers her hands to my hips, rocking them to the music. I put mine on her shoulders, keeping my eyes on her gyrations. As a stripper, she's got the moves. But after a few minutes my body responds to the beat and I let go of my mentor. A few minutes more, and I'm dancing around her as though it's second nature. Every time I feel self-conscious, my eyes dart around but no one is staring at me and laughing. No one is imitating me. Some dance with closed eyes. Others swirl round and round. The people here don't seem to care what anyone else is doing or how they do it. They left their judgments at the door.

The more time that passes, the freer I feel, letting my body move whatever way it wants.

Soon after my mind shuts off and my body takes over, euphoria sets in. Everything falls away, replaced by fluid movements, silken flesh, and sweaty chaos. I've never felt this free, not even tumbling down from six stories up. Why did I let

Justine Miller win all those years ago, robbing me of this outlet, this blissful escape from reality? Her human family left the Edge not long after that dance so many moons ago, but she never really left, did she? I carried her in my heart, locked up deep inside, in a place I couldn't reach. I carried the doubt and uncertainty that she left for me. I carried that lie, from middle school until the present day. Unburdening myself of it is the exact metamorphosis I needed to transcend.

And, oh, how I soar. "Thank you, Rhys," I whisper.

Oblivious of my surroundings, I spin in circles, laughter bubbling up from the deepest and darkest places of my soul. Arms circle my waist, lifting me up and up, toward the ceiling. Enjoying Burgundy's vampire strength, I hold my arms out to the sides, twirling, eyes closed. Around and around until I'm laughing so hard tears stream down my face. As my body is lowered, my eyes flicker open and my feet touch the floor. I spin around to smile at Burg, but it isn't Burg holding me up. It is Rhys, my fulcrum. My anchor. Thorn and Dominic throw their arms around me, too, drowning me in a ferocious hug. I throw my arms around them as well and we spin together, sparks flying madly through the night.

CHAPTER TWELVE

THORN

*W*atching Iphigenia dance is like watching the sun dip below a cloudy horizon. The light this girl—this *woman* brings to those around her is almost too bright to watch, but she gilds everything around her in beauty and life. Her curls fan out around her in a halo as she throws herself, headlong, fearless, into a dance. She amazes me—and my brothers. They've all vowed to keep her safe from *him* and though I pretend not to care, I'm beyond gone on her as well.

Keeping my feelings in check is my play for keeping our pack in check. Jealousy and pettiness could break us apart.

They've all talked about this while I've sat stoically, listening. Pretending not to be attracted to her. They agreed that if she chose one of them, the others would respect her choice. I just hope it *is* one of them and not some undeserving asshole outside of our pack.

I want it to be me, but there's no way it will be. I haven't shown the slightest bit of interest. If anything, she probably thinks I don't even like her. That couldn't be farther from the truth. And if she knew I'd developed feelings for her, she'd run as fast as possible to the other side of the Edge. Just like every other woman I've let get close to me in the past. And that was without any of them knowing what I'm capable of.

Iphigenia's smile and laughter pull me up from my darkness. That angry black hole where my killer lives. She whites out the haunting visions of a blackened corpse, her bubbly personality dousing my memories, my anger, my fire. I want more. I want to touch her. She hasn't chosen any of them yet and if I don't make at least one play, I'll have no one to blame but myself.

So when Rhys approaches her on the dance floor, I don't stop myself. I cut in front of him. It's a dick move but I don't care. Grasping her waist, I lift her high and spin her. Around and around, watching her fly, that flaxen hair billowing through the air.

The bodies around us move to the rhythm. Beautiful women and men clutch one another or dance alone, their bodies slick with sweat. A feast for the eyes. One girl removes her top and throws it high in the air, big tits bouncing, and still, I'm not interested. I only have eyes for Iphi, even if she doesn't know it, and I'm glad she's not showing the club her goods. But I beat back the caveman routine. Such small-minded thoughts have no place here.

The surge of protectiveness is hard to suppress, though, hardwired in me as it is. I'm not proud of what I had to do to make sure our pack survived, but we all do what we have to, especially when we don't know how to do anything else. Too late for me, I now know there are other ways. Iphi is the youngest of her clan yet she's the fierce protector of her two older sisters and even her mother, and she does it with kindness, hope, and acceptance. Clan first. Pack first. Family first.

"How long have you all been here?" Iphi's breath tickles my ear. Her scent, even in a room filled with the stench of sweat, perfume, and Lycra, wafts up like lilacs on a fresh summer breeze.

"Long enough to watch you dance."

She blushes, turning to run away. Dominic catches her easily, his arms circling her tiny waist as he spins her to Rhys, who spins her back to me. We dance like this for a while, each of us taking a turn, each of us spinning her to the next.

Maybe it's like spin the bottle and she'll stop on one of us when she chooses. But who will it be?

"Hey, handsome," Burgundy growls in my ear. The beautiful vampire is swaying her voluptuous hips and tossing her thick dark hair, trying to entice me to dance with her. "There's only one Iphi and three of you. Surely I can have one for a dance?"

Burgundy and I are not friends but we know of each other. I've gone diving with her lovers, and we're friends in that way only people who've faced danger together can be. Itching for adventure, I booked them for a dive in Ginnie Springs, Florida. There's a labyrinth of caves there, most of them named after the devil. In this ghastly vortex in Devil's Ear, I forged the way ahead while Tiyah had to hold on to Elijah. Something I've never let them live down.

Burgundy seems cool, but— "I'm here to dance with Iphigenia."

"Suit yourself." She smiles. "I can't say I blame you. That girl is a ball of light."

"In a pitch-black night," I add.

Burgundy rolls her eyes, then leans in. "Just don't hurt her. Any of you. Or I'll have to kill you." And with that, she dances away.

If anyone hurts her, I will kill them, I want to scream over the music.

Iphi shimmies toward me, her hips dipping with every beat of the music. Standing on tiptoe, she puts her arms around my neck, her hips twisting against mine. I try, unsuccessfully, to hide my raging hard-on.

When she bumps against it, her eyes widen. I shrug, and she giggles before dancing up to Rhys and smiling slyly up at him.

Exchanging glances with my brothers, I motion to the bathroom and hold up a finger, moving off by myself to take care of business. So intent am I on getting my gonads under control that I don't see the tiny brunette slinking toward me until I've entered the bathroom. When I turn to close and lock the door on the unisex room, the girl stands there, her back against the already closed door, trapping me inside with her. Without saying a word, she tears off her halter top. And even though I'm a man starved for female attention right now, I don't want her. She's not the right woman. The right woman is still dancing outside with my brothers.

"Miss . . . ?"

"Courtney," she purrs.

"Courtney, you are lovely, no doubt about it—"

"Thank you. Come take some then. Or if you'd rather . . . ?" She raises her brows at me.

"I apologize, Courtney, but I only have eyes for another."

"That doesn't seem to be stopping you." She eyes the bulge in my pants, then takes a step closer. "I can take care of that. I *want* to take care of that."

Before I can move, the woman drops to her knees in front of my package, reaching for the zipper of my leather pants.

Grabbing her wrists, I hold her still, gentle, but implacable. "I said I'm not interested." My eyes hold hers until she looks away, a faint red flushing her cheeks.

"What man says no to head?" she mumbles, pulling her hands away from me, and stumbling to her feet.

"This has nothing to do with you," I grate. "I told you, my heart belongs to another." I'm used to my bulk making people cower, which is why I'm trying to be gentle with her. Unfortunately, she takes my kindness as an invitation despite my words and presses her body against mine. I'm a hetero man and my body can't help but respond to her, my bulge straining against the leather. Her arms wrap around my neck in the same way Iphi's did only moments ago. Her bare breasts rub up and down my T-shirt and she nuzzles my neck with her nose. I've wrapped my hands around her waist and am tugging her away when the door opens.

"Oh." Iphi's voice is high and breathy, tinged with sadness. "I didn't realize you were . . . engaged. Sorry." The door closes softly and I bite back a curse.

CHAPTER THIRTEEN

IPHIGENIA

blink rapidly, trying to rid myself of the scene I just witnessed. Drunk on the music, adrenaline, and freedom, I followed Thorn to the back, wanting to know just how he'd take care of his erection. And whether he wanted help. But someone beat me to it.

And what of it? Thorn is a man free to make love to any woman. I want to be happy for him, that this beautiful, petite, topless brunette was pressed up against him.

But . . . I'm not happy. The girl who is happy for everyone. The girl who prides herself on never judging others. For once, the role chafes, strangling me in my own skin.

I rush around Promise, not dancing, eyes unable to focus on the throngs of bodies gyrating to the music. What the hell was I thinking? Where is Burgundy? The other guys? I need to get that picture out of my mind.

"Iphigenia?"

I whirl around to face him, those dark eyes clouded with something I can't identify.

"I'm sorry, Thorn." I turn away. I can't look at him and I don't know what to say past that.

"What are you sorry for? I'm the one who's sorry." He touches my chin with just one finger, enticing my gaze back up. The intensity in his eyes finally blocks out the image of that girl.

"Why are you—" But his head leans down and my own strains up to meet his. Our lips touch and before that moment, I hadn't realized how much I wanted this. Him. The taste of him sears through my core, like a rope wrapped too tightly around my body as I drop to a stage a thousand feet below. Except this burning, his heat, is the opposite of painful. I let him take my mouth, unable to hold back a moan as I mold myself to his body. His arms fold around me, pulling me tighter while his tongue darts out, parting my lips. Painfully slow, he licks them, tracing each contour, and I lean my head back, gasping for air. Thorn mistakes my movement and steps back, leaving only a hand on my shoulder as I wobble on my feet.

"Iphigenia, are you okay?"

"I think so." I'm trembling and confused. I want more of this man, but I also feel torn. What about Rhys? Caspian? How can I want all three? And what will they do when they find out?

"There you are." Rhys moves next to me, reaching for my hand as if I called him out of the ether with my thoughts. Bending down, he brushes a strand of hair off my cheek and kisses me there.

I shake my head at him and then at Thorn. Pulling my hand out of Rhys's grasp, I turn and run through the club until I spot my friend dancing with her lovers.

"Burgundy."

"Iphi, what's happened? Did someone try to hurt you?"

I shake my head. "I want to go home. Can you take me?"

"Of course." She holds on to my arm, leaning in to whisper to her lovers. They nod and smile, waving her off.

~ ❖ �֍ ❖ ~

I follow her to the car and climb into the passenger seat.

"Do you really want to go home?"

I shake my head.

"How about some dessert?"

With a wobbly smile, I climb back out of Cherry and we walk to Confections. I blink against the bright lights inside, a welcome contrast to the darkness outside and the dim lights in Promise. "Can we sit in the back?"

She leads, passing a cluster of high school kids giggling around a pile of ice cream sundaes.

Finding a back booth, she slides in. "Do you want to grab something first?"

"Yeah. My treat. What do you want?"

"Tres leches cake, please, and a cup of coffee." She grins and I cluck my tongue. Why did I even ask?

After I grab a slice of cake and a coffee for her and that amazing apple fritter for me, I return and take the seat next to her.

She cuts to the chase. "Did something happen at Promise that upset you?"

I nod, sucking on a spoonful of apple sugar. "I don't know what's going on with me or those men."

She cocks her head, spearing a bite of her cake with her fork.

"I have feelings for them."

She drops the fork as a mad grin overtakes her face. "All of them?"

"Not all, but more than one. How can that be? And what should I do? I mean, how do I choose?"

"Why choose?"

I hold up a finger. "One, I doubt they're going to want to share." I add my middle finger. "Two, what would people say?" I tap my ring finger. "Three, how would I juggle them?" I hold up my pinky. "And four, my mother would disown me."

"Are you asking me or telling me?"

"I have no idea what the hell I'm doing right now." I drop my head into my hands.

"Sweetie," she peels one of my hands back, "what if there were no boundaries around this? What if . . ." She holds up her index finger. "They were fine with sharing you." She holds up her next one. "No one else cared." She holds up her third finger. "There is no juggling; it just works." She holds up her pinky. "Aurelia is not part of this equation."

I sigh and bite the inside of my cheek. "What's it like being in a relationship with two people at the same time?"

"So you *are* interested in being in a thruple? With two of the hotties?" Rubbing her hands together she leans toward me. "Which ones?"

The heat in my face intensifies. "I'm just curious."

"That would be so perfect for you, Iphigenia. I can totally see it."

I roll my eyes and hold my thick hair up off the back of my neck. Between my Rex impression on the way to Promise and all the dancing, I don't think there's a single bobby pin left. I fan myself with a hand. "I'm not even going to ask why you think I could do it. I just wonder how you do."

"Are you asking about sexually? In the bedroom? Who's on top and that sort of thing?"

"Very funny." I roll my eyes at her and take another bite of my dessert. "What about the difficulty of it all? The challenges?"

"No more than your usual couple challenges. There needs to be a lot of open communication and no hidden feelings, that's the biggest part."

"And," I wave my hand around the restaurant, "what about them?"

"Them?" She licks her fork suggestively. "Ahh, you're asking about what other people think and say?"

I nod.

"Screw 'em. People will judge no matter what you do. It's in their nature. They will judge what you choose to do with your life and they'll find you wanting. They won't agree with your choices, even if they would have made the same choices themselves." She barks out a laugh. "Especially then."

"But why?"

"You know why." She takes a sip of coffee. "They're jealous or insecure or too set in their ways, mostly. It usually stems from one of those. But Iphi, they get to live their lives and you get to live yours. This is the life you get to live, if you choose."

"You make it sound so easy." I pick apart a piece of apple with my fingers, the rich dessert suddenly hard to swallow.

She laughs, deep, rich, right from her belly. "Relationships are never easy. They take a lot of work, constantly, but they're worth it. Living the life you choose, on the other hand, is easy. But you have to want it and I don't know if you're there yet." She shrugs and eats more of her cake.

"There you are," comes a soft voice from behind us. "And you're eating my favorite dessert." Caspian slides in next to me and picks a piece of apple off my plate.

My heart lurches and then free falls all the way to my feet. This is what I was dreaming of and here it is, with the man who almost died because of me.

I throw my arms around him and bury my face in the warmth of his neck, nuzzling in between his shoulder and his hair. "What are you doing here? Shouldn't you be resting?"

"I had to make sure that Thorn didn't steal you away when I wasn't watching."

Heat crawls up my cheeks. Caspian places his large hand over mine and leans in, his warm breath tickling my ear. "Mmmm, you smell like Thorn. I don't mind that you made out with him," he whispers and the heat of his voice shoots sparks of warm pleasure through my arms and legs. Zap. Zap. Zap. "Rhys fixed me all up before everyone left to meet you but I needed a little more time to rest and shower."

He places a bite of apple into my mouth, watching as I suck the candied fruit and syrup off his fingers. His pale-blue eyes, bright like moonlight, meet mine and he catches my bottom lip between his teeth. My body and mind are no longer connected and I let myself go for the second time that night. Lost in the moment, I tumble head over feet in an aerial free fall with no mat below to bounce off of, no net to catch me, and no sense left in my own head to pull away.

CHAPTER FOURTEEN

IPHIGENIA

*M*y body is still ringing with Caspian's kiss when the five of us stand outside together a few minutes later. I'm hardly able to look at Thorn or Caspian. At least Dominic is still inside and not here to dissect me with his gaze again.

"We'll make sure she gets home safely," Rhys says to Burgundy. "You go back and dance with your darlings."

Burgundy holds up a finger and pulls me aside. "I won't leave you unless you want to be left."

Instead of answering, I look between her and the men, biting my lip.

"You want my advice?" she asks. "I won't give it if you don't."

I nod.

"Go for it. Stop overthinking everything and *look*. There are no fisticuffs happening here." She motions toward the guys. It's true, they're all standing around talking, laughing, and ribbing each other like brothers, not like men about to brawl over one indecisive woman. "Let go."

"I don't know if I can."

Burgundy shrugs one shoulder. "Then it'll be your loss."

I squint at her. It's too much pressure. How does she know it'll be my loss anyway? I've never even had one real boyfriend. How could I have three?

"Do you want me to take you home then?" she asks.

"No, you go back to Promise and enjoy yourself."

"I really hope you're making the choice to go with them because you want to and not because you don't want to inconvenience me."

Am I that transparent? "Go." I shoo her away and turn back to the men. "Okay, boys, which one of you is taking me home?"

They all raise their hands, which makes me laugh.

"You choose," says Thorn, his dark eyes flashing.

Does he want me to choose him? After tonight, there's no question he's interested in me, too. My head is about to explode from all this male attention and confusion.

"I can't," I say, not wanting to hurt anyone's feelings.

"All right, we'll each make our case," says Rhys. "If you pick me, I'll give you a back rub."

"Oh, man, so unfair," says Caspian. "That's my specialty."

"I'll take you on a long motorcycle ride through the hills or hang-gliding over the beach," says Thorn.

Caspian growls. "Fine. If you pick me, you can do whatever you want, whenever you want. If you want to go sailing or scuba diving, I'll take you. If you want a romantic picnic on the beach, I'll make that happen. A foot or scalp rub, I'm your man. Your choice, seraphim."

Holding my arms out to the sides I spin in circles on the boardwalk, throwing my head back and laughing. "What if I pick all of you?" I ask, just to see what they'll say.

"Then you'll get it all," says Rhys, scooping me up in his arms and spinning me around before passing me to Caspian, who does the same, and then passes me to Thorn. My feet never touch the ground as all three of them spin me, arms held wide.

When they finally put me down, I'm giggling so hard I have to lean on Thorn's massive bulk. "Seriously, though, right now you do have to choose because we took separate cars," he says.

I look from one man to the next, not wanting to leave anyone out, and my gaze settles on Rhys. If somehow I get caught by Aurelia, at least it'll be with a man she knows. I cannot imagine her reaction to any of the others. She would seriously lose her shit and turn us all into rats or toads or something. She's done it before.

Rhys takes my hand. "Sorry, losers," he calls to the others but I break away from him to hug each of the guys, starting with Thorn. I press my body close to him, then Caspian, trying not to pant when moisture pools between my legs. Turning away from them isn't easy.

I take Rhys's hand again and he leads me down the pier, into a parking lot, and to his Thunderbird. Unlocking the door for me, he holds it open until I slide in.

"So where can I give you that back rub?"

⌐ ◇ ❁ ◇ ¬

*M*y window is still open with the screen off and I let out a long sigh of relief. Rhys's hands are around my waist, lifting me up to the sill. Clamoring in as quietly as I can, I reach my hand back out to help him through but he waves it away, crouches, and jumps through the window. He lands with a soft thud on my bedroom floor. How do I keep forgetting he's a vampire? Impressive.

"Impressive," he says, but he's talking about my room.

My face warms but for the first time I'm glad I never had a typical little girl's room. My sisters used to make fun of me but I always suspected they were a tad jealous that my taste grew up faster than theirs. Or maybe that's just what I told myself to keep from feeling completely different. While my peers stuffed their spaces overnight with pallets of IKEA furniture, I saved and scrimped for real pieces, adding one precious antique at a time, starting with my mahogany four-poster bed. *So there, Rhys. Here's something I did all for me.*

"Shall we get started?" Rhys whispers, so close to my hair it sends tingles down my spine.

This is the first time in my entire life that I'm actually doing something very wrong in my mother's house. Sneaking out was bad enough, but now I've brought a man home to touch me. But where else can I go? Surely, Mother would rather Rhys give me a massage in the safety of my own house than, say, some skeezy motel room.

Keeping my sundress on, I remove my shoes, pull back the covers, and push aside the pillows I had propped there for the spell. Lying on my bed face-down, I let out a shaky breath.

Thankfully, he doesn't tell me to remove my dress, but a moment later he's straddling me and I let out a little squeal.

"Shit. Am I too heavy or does this make you uncomfortable?" he asks.

"No. You just surprised me. Go ahead."

Rhys's strong hands push over the back of my sundress, kneading the skin underneath. The only massages I've ever had were at the circus, sitting on a chair, but even so I know you aren't supposed to have a full-body one over clothing.

"Hey, lemme get up for a minute," I say and he jumps off. "You're not supposed to do it over cloth-ing, right?"

"There's no 'supposed to,'" he says. "It's what you're comfortable with."

"Stay there." I go into my closet and rummage around for something more revealing, yet comfort-able. I slip on a backless dress of simple cotton, then return to the bed. "How's this?"

"Whatever you choose, I'll work with. It's about your pleasure, but yes, that's great."

Smiling at him, I hop back on the bed and resume my position.

"Do you mind if I use some of this lotion?" He

points at the rose body cream sitting on my bedside table.

"Just don't get it on my dress."

"I'll try, but no promises." He squeezes some into his palm and then rubs it on my back.

I melt into my soft mattress topper and the air leaves my lungs. His big hands slide over my back, pressing against all my sore muscles.

"Wow, you're really strong." His voice is deeper now and a little hoarse. "Can I move the straps aside to reach your shoulders?"

"Sure." I wriggle my arms to help and he moves the spaghetti straps over my shoulders and down my arms.

He starts on my shoulders, rubbing in small circles, expertly pressing on all the sore spots. Clutching my biceps, he squeezes them, clicking his tongue, which makes me giggle. Those rough hands return to the top of my shoulders, then lower, kneading the knots below my shoulder blades. My body melts further into my topper.

"You're really good at this," I murmur as actual drool escapes the corner of my mouth. It's okay, he can't see it. As the soothing, rhythmic strokes continue, I get sleepier and sleepier, letting my eyes drift shut.

CHAPTER FIFTEEN

IPHIGENIA

he sense of being watched, and not in a good way, forces my eyes open wide. Where am I? It's my bedroom but all my furniture is gone, save my bed. Where has it all gone? There's an eerie cast to everything, as though shadows are walking up the walls. Lurking.

Shivering, I reach for the light on my bedside table but it's not there and neither is the table. There's a scratching at my window and I hold my breath. Where did Rhys go? Is that him outside? Throwing my legs over the bed, I stand and putter to my curtains, pulling them aside.

And scream.

Pressed against every pane are hungry vampires with red eyes and long claws, scratching and scratching. Shrieking even louder, I run to my bedroom door and yank on the doorknob. But it doesn't budge. I'm locked in? With monsters trying to reach me?

"Mother, help!" I shriek as loudly as I can. She'll know what to do. I cower at my door, sinking down in front of it, trying to make myself smaller, and closing my eyes.

Suddenly my body is covered with hands and claws, scraping at my skin. I have no time to wonder how these monsters got inside before I sit straight up, screaming, my eyes flying open.

Disoriented, I blink in the dim light. I'm in my room still, but now everything is where it should be, where it's supposed to be.

Everything except for the vampires, that is. They are here, too. In my bedroom. In the light, they're even less human looking, pawing and scratching at my bedsheets. Shredding them. They're drooling and hollow-eyed and so far from Burg or Carter or Rhys it's like they're not even the same species anymore. I count six and pinch myself over and over again to wake up from the nightmare within the nightmare. Except that I can feel the bite of each pinch stinging my flesh, and angry red welts appear. The vampires claw my bedsheets but they don't touch me, hovering just out of reach. My amulet. I clutch it and scream for Mother.

The door handle to my room jiggles but doesn't open.

"Iphigenia, let me in this instant!" Aurelia calls out from the other side. "What's going on in there?"

"Vampires! Mother, please help. They're trying to attack me!"

She pounds on the door, jiggling the handle, but it remains closed and I don't dare get up.

Alistair's deep voice reaches inside. "That's not possible; you must be having a lucid dream."

"This is no dream!" I yell, scrambling as far away from them as I can.

"Iphigenia," a female vampire hisses. I don't recognize her. The only one I recognize is my neighbor, the same one I saw get bitten. By Nolan.

"Who are you? What do you want?" I shriek.

"The eyes of another watch you. Through mine. He will make you his," she whispers.

"Stop fighting," says a male vampire.

"There's no escape," whispers a third.

"Come," a woman motions to me with her arms, "join us."

Outside my room, it sounds like Alistair is throwing his whole body against my bedroom door over and over again. I'm absolutely terrified but I can't move and I know they can't touch me.

"Get the hell out of my room!" I yell. "Leave me alone!"

They laugh, together, a shrill cackling that raises the hairs on the back of my neck.

Something whooshes outside my window. All of our heads turn in unison to look. It can't be. I've never seen anything like it before. A very small dragon, about the size of a large hawk, hangs in the air, its wings flapping. I laugh. I must be dreaming after all.

"Why are you laughing!" demands Mother from outside my room.

"I *am* dreaming."

"Are you mad?"

"Quite likely," I admit as the miniature dragon flies through my window.

"No!" a deep male voice booms. The sound is elongated, hollow, distant.

The dragon opens its mouth and a stream of fire erupts, torching one of the vampires. En masse, they all scramble toward the open window, leaping out one after the other.

"Stop!" I scream, holding up my hands. I'm afraid this creature will burn me alive or set my room on fire and I'll be trapped.

The lizard head turns toward me and blinks once, hovering in the air. Those eyes—vertical pupils, jagged and edged with black scales. Familiar, though I know no one with eyes like them. The thing lands on my bed and I'm scrambling back, feeling around for a weapon, when it makes a disarming whirring noise. And then it lays its head down. Cute. I reach one unsteady hand toward it, studying the thing. It looks even more like a very large lizard now that its wings are tucked against its back. The face is long and thin with little spikes running down the back of its head. Its skin and wings are tinged red. He opens his eyes and blinks once at me, and familiarity turns to recognition. It *could* be any one of them, since I only know two of Caspian's shifts, but no. This is Thorn.

"Thorn?" I whisper and he makes that whirring, chirping noise again, rolling over onto his back. Smiling, I pet his leathery tummy. "Thank you," I say. And then my bedroom door opens, and Mother stands there with narrowed eyes, her hands on her hips.

"What the hell is going on here?" But she doesn't wait for a response before throwing a hand toward Thorn. *"Rigescunt indutae."*

Thorn takes flight, even with the freeze spell she just cast, but his motions are jerky and slow. He makes it out the window, Mother chasing him.

She slams it closed behind her, drawing a

pentacle with her finger and incanting more Latin. Her words will keep anyone from entering my room, good or bad. I'm terrified of the vampires. But what about my shifters and Rhys?

Whirling to face me, Mother moves her hands to her hips. "You are in trouble, young lady."

"What? Why?" I scramble to my feet.

"Lying about vampires, burning your bed with that . . . that . . . miscreant." She sniffs. "I'm sure there are other things I just haven't caught you at yet," she surveys my room, "from the look of things."

"Mother, six vampires crawled through my room and tried to kill me. That shifter saved my life."

"Liar!" she screams, pointing her finger at me. "I know you're not always completely forthcoming, Iphigenia, but I never thought you were an outright liar. You sure had me fooled."

"Look in your crystal ball then. That doesn't lie."

"Darling," Alistair's hand is on her shoulder, "whatever happened here, Iphi needs her rest now and so do we. Are you going to be all right?" he asks me.

I bite my lip, fighting back tears, and nod.

"Leave your door open," Mother huffs, then leaves the room with her gentleman vampire trailing behind her.

"Call us if you need anything," he says on his way out.

Yeah, right. So I can be accused of lying again? I pull my sheets up—the top half isn't burned—and hold them to my face, stopping the flow of tears. I'm not even safe in my mother's house? My house? The shifters came to my rescue again. And who were the vampires talking about? Nolan? Couldn't be, he said he was being controlled by another, too. The one who spoke through him. There is only one being I've ever encountered in my life who could do that—the Scrim. But we banished him back to his dimension. My father did. He gave his freedom and maybe his life to save us, to save the world. But if there is one evil entity like the Scrim, why can't there be more?

*A*fter Mother leaves, I change my sheets, hoping she'll confirm what happened in her crystal ball. Of all the times for her *not* to cast a truth spell. Does she fear the truth so much?

I text Rhys to see if Thorn is all right but don't hear back. He's probably sleeping. It is three in the morning. It's difficult for me to fall asleep but I finally do.

When I open my eyes again, light streams

through my window and there's a furious knock on my door. Before I can answer, the door slams open and Mother stands in the doorway, her reddish hair swirling around her like a mad witch, no less furious than last night.

"Why is your door closed? And why didn't you come to breakfast?"

I look around my room, my heart pounding in my head. The windows are all closed, my sheer gauzy drapes drawn.

"I forgot. I got up to go to the bathroom and then I crashed again. I'm sorry, I overslept."

Aurelia sniffs, narrows her eyes, and looks around my room as well. "Fine. Put on your robe and come out now. Breakfast is ready."

"Yes, Mother." I leap out of bed and run to my closet, grabbing my robe while she waits at the door, unmoving.

I slip into my house shoes and fly past her and into the dining room, forcing her to follow.

"Did you have a chance to check your crystal ball?" I ask.

"I did, but it stayed clear, so unless you pissed off another witch, you were indeed lying." Her eyes narrow.

Taking my seat, I put my elbows on the table and drop my head into my hands. Suddenly it's pounding, like silks are wrapped around my neck, cutting off the air to my brain. "Why would I make up something so elaborate?" I ask her through my fingers.

"Young lady," she snaps as she slips into her seat at the head of the table, "manners." Her eyes dart to my elbows and I remove them.

I help myself to a waffle. "There's something seriously strange going on. Those vampires were out for blood."

My mother exchanges a look with Alistair.

"We're not saying we don't believe what you saw last night," he says kindly. "But maybe it was a nightmare, or maybe you had a fever. I told your mother that I think you should go see the doctor, make sure you're fine. What if it was a hallucination?"

I slam my fists on the table, causing them both to jump.

"That was not a hallucination. Six vampires were trying to kill me and someone else was controlling them. What if the Scrim is back?"

A strangled sound escapes from the back of Mother's throat. "Why would you suggest such a thing?" She looks at Alistair and then back at me. "Are you upset about our relationship?"

"What? No. Of course not." I look between them. "This has nothing to do with the two of you. Or Dad."

"Do not speak of your father." Her eyes mist and she turns away.

"It's okay, darling, I want Iphi to be comfortable enough in front of me to talk about anything."

"Not him," she hisses. "Never him."

I clench my jaw and stuff a bite of waffle into my mouth, chewing noisily.

"Manners," Aurelia barks. "We do not chew with our mouths open."

Why chew at all? Her normally delicious breakfast suddenly tastes like cardboard in my mouth. I take a long sip of water to wash down the chalky substance, then stand up, and walk out of the dining room. Aurelia yells at me to come back and sit down but I don't.

CHAPTER SIXTEEN

IPHIGENIA

*L*ater that evening, I'm still reeling from the attack—both of them, really. My mother's disbelief hurts far more than the failed vampire attack. My worry for Thorn doesn't help. Rhys finally texted, saying there was an issue but that Thorn wasn't hurt. Whatever that meant. What did that mean?

All this drama, worry, and pre-show adrenaline makes applying eyeliner to my already overly made-up face a dangerous endeavor. It's a wonder I don't poke out my own eye.

Rodrigo peeks into my dressing room. "You ready to go on in five?"

"Of course." I haven't even put my costume on yet.

"Wearing your bathrobe?"

"I'll be ready," I snap, and he straightens. "Sorry. I'm sorry. I'm on edge. No excuse. Can you buy me an extra two minutes?"

"No problem," he calls, already walking away.

I don't have time to beat myself up for snapping at Rodrigo, but it's not like me. I pride myself on my unflappable, professional demeanor.

Is Rhys out there? And the rest of the men? When I asked him if they were coming to my show, he said they'd try. Not knowing is worse than if he'd just told me no.

They really have no reason to come back tonight. I perform the same act every night of the season, and they've already seen it. And yet . . . *Focus. Concentrate.* Aerial is not something you want to do when your mind is elsewhere.

"Tonight you're in for a treat. Our amazing Iphigenia, the Flying Seraphim, will be performing a brand-new silks act, never before seen. Put your hands together and welcome our young phenom to the stage!" Alexis bleats into the microphone.

Applause sounds and I push through the center curtain to strike a pose in front of the fabric. Willing myself not to check the audience, visually or mentally, I wait for the music and begin. The climb up morphs into slow motion, hand over hand, no legs. One hand up and grab, then pull. Over and over, my legs stretched down and held together, my toes pointed. With my sparkling green-and-blue tights, the effect is supposed to be that of a mermaid. After a full day of hurt, worry, and confusion, going through my routine finally quiets the noise in my head. Everything falls away. The music, the crowd, my ego.

I've been practicing contortion for the past several years in order to get the most out of my static aerial poses, and it's paid off. Arching backward, one hand on the silks, I'm able to touch my leg to the top of my head and hold my other arm out in a backward ouroboros. Faintly, I can hear the crowd roar, but it's so easy to tune them all out.

After my final drop and double salto landing, I allow myself a peek at the house. But all I see are strangers. The front row is filled with people I don't recognize, and beyond them, no one stands out in the crowd. Not my admirers, not my sisters, certainly not my mother. I toss my head, plaster a fake smile on my face, and take a bow.

Backstage, I run to my dressing room. My body feels like a loose balloon, devoid of all oxygen. My bones ache as if they've been pummeled by a hammer and my eyes sting as I fight back the tears.

Pull yourself together. You've still got the finale to perform. I've been performing every summer for the past three years. I can't expect everyone I know to come to every show.

"You were amazing."

I spin around. Caspian is here, taking up the entire doorway.

Caspian

a smile breaks across her face and grows impossibly larger when I push into her dressing room, followed quickly by Dominic and Rhys.

A low whistle escapes my lips, and the three of us line up in front of her.

Her head cranes, trying to look past us, and then she crosses her arms over her chest. "Where's Thorn? And where were you three? Did you arrive late?"

We men exchange looks.

"We didn't want to distract you, so we watched from the back," Dominic says.

"Well, you did distract me," she huffs and Rhys punches Dominic in the arm.

"Hey," he cries out, "what was that for?"

"Distracting Iphigenia by trying not to distract her," he says. He's so serious I can't help but laugh.

"I wanted to know you were here. I *needed* to know you were here. Is Thorn in the restroom?"

"We wouldn't have missed it," I say, trying to change the subject.

"Well, move to the front for the finale, please," she sniffs.

"Done," says Dominic.

"We don't want to muss your outfit, but can we hug you for forgiveness?" Rhys's dark eyes smolder when she bobs her head in assent.

Wow. He possesses an undeniable smoothness that mirrors the beauty of a painted sunset, enchanting her with his vibrancy and infectious smile.

Before I can jump in, Rhys has wrapped his arms around her and she leans into him, standing on her tiptoes to press her face into his neck and inhale. A large smile breaks over my face and my eyes moisten at her obvious happiness. So carefree and present. Locked in a moment with him. My contentment for her, for them both is a welcome relief from the worry that cropped up earlier. She is well taken care of, by us all.

Rhys gently lets her go, spinning her to the left where I catch and hold her tightly. What a fun game.

I take my Iphi moment by circling my arms about her waist, touching her there with my hands, and lifting her up. She was already on her tiptoes but I raise her to my face and rub my nose against hers, letting that beatific smile bathe my soul in sunlight.

"So this is why you never wanted me to come watch you perform?" Aurelia's shrill voice pierces our moment of bliss. I put Iphigenia down and a hush descends as if all the air has been sucked out of the too-small dressing room.

"Mother!"

I bow to her stiffly. "Mrs. Holt."

Rhys flinches. "*Ms.* Holt."

Iphigenia

"*I*'m so glad you're h-here," I stammer. She finally came to see me perform! My chest puffs with pride over my performance, then deflates. Oh, Goddess, what she just witnessed in my dressing room . . .

"This is what I get for surprising you?" Her voice is stiff.

"I— No, I mean, I just can't believe you came to a performance. You've never—"

"And now I know why you've never encouraged me to do so before."

My stomach lurches. I've wanted so much for her to come to my performances, but I always made allowances for her fear and her helicopter parenting, and now putting her first is coming back to slap me in the face. "What? I'm over the moon that you're here. I just wasn't expecting you."

"Obviously not, or you wouldn't be acting like a little tart, I suppose." She motions around the small space at the men standing there, staring at her. "Or maybe that's exactly who you are, a little slut just like your sisters."

"Mama, no." At this moment, I'd rather be auditioning in front of Cirque du Soleil's entire cast with no rehearsal first. And no clothes. What must the men think of me? Caspian looks like he's swallowed something foul. Rhys's fists are white with strain. And Dominic . . . His face is blank. Withdrawn. Judging?

She holds her hand up. "You're right, Iphigenia, you're nothing like them. You're worse than they are. At least they didn't try to hide it, to pretend they were something they were not. Unlike you. How duplicitous."

My chest tightens as though I've been stabbed, not just shamed.

"Ms. Holt," Rhys holds up a hand, "Iphi is the kindest and most loving person that any of us have ever met."

Aurelia snorts. "Compared to the tarts you men usually surround yourselves with, I'm sure that's true."

Rhys looks like he wants to say more, but I raise a hand. It's sweet, but this isn't about them. Or me. It's about Aurelia.

She takes the interruption as her due and barrels on. "Why would you hurt me like this? After your siblings crushed me, after you promised not to do the same?" Her voice raises an octave and her hands shake. "Please, Iphigenia, be the bigger person. Say goodbye to your boyfriends and come back home. Haven't you been happy with me and Alistair?"

Unable to control my tongue, as if it has a mind of its own, I whisper, "No, Mom, I haven't." Once it's out, I know it to be true. What's been said can't be unsaid, denied, or revoked.

Her beautiful face crumples behind her hands.

My heart cracks inside my chest. I want to throw myself at her and cry but now is the time to hold my ground. "Mama, all I've ever wanted was to make you proud but in doing so, I lost myself."

Her nostrils flare. "Selfish girl, just like Sadie and

Chrys, putting yourself and your needs first. No different." Her voice cracks and she turns to leave.

"Mother, please," I cry. "I've never wanted to hurt you!"

"Too late," she sobs and walks out the door.

A wave of nausea courses through my stomach but I swallow it down. Rhys rushes to my side and I sag into his grip. His hand is on the back of my head, crushing me to his broad chest as the tears pour out. If I weren't so distraught, I'd be embarrassed, breaking down in front of them, but in moments, all of their arms are around me, holding me, petting my head, and whispering into my ears.

The sensations overwhelm me but not my grief. I've always prided myself on my strength. I am the person others come to for help and support, even my own mother. I was the one who helped her navigate the waters of a new relationship. The one who comforted her when first one, then two of her daughters left her. The one who picked up the pieces after Father took off with a demon. It's all too much, this responsibility. Who takes care of me? Who's ever taken care of me? My breath comes in gasps and the men are pushing me down. Why? I struggle against them, but a thick film slides across my vision.

"Slow your breathing down," one of the men says but I don't know who.

"Is there a paper bag anywhere?" another shouts. "Get her a paper bag."

"Don't let her head hit the . . ."

CHAPTER SEVENTEEN

IPHIGENIA

*M*y mouth is dry and I'm shivering. My body feels like it belongs to someone else, as though I'm merely a ghost inhabiting a shell. I crack open my eyes, then slam them shut again. So bright. Where am I? In a soft bed, but not my own. Sitting up too quickly, I hit my head on a low ceiling. I rub the sore spot and then my aching temples. Such a deep ache, too, one that stretches farther than the confines of my body, like tendrils of rope reaching up and into the ether.

A knock sounds on an unfamiliar door. "Come in." I shimmy onto my belly to peek down out of the loft.

The door below me cracks open just a sliver and Dominic pokes his head in. He props open the door and pushes inside, carrying a tray laden with food. Delicious scents waft up into the loft.

The space below me looks like a little den. The room is cozy with a pot bellied stove, dark wooden walls, and furniture. There's a rustic brown leather couch and two brown leather chairs that remind me of the type you'd see in a therapist's office.

"Where am I?"

"Do you want me to come up there?" he asks.

Goddess, no. I'm not sure I even want him to come in. But he's radiating nothing but calm concern. "No, I'll come down."

"How are you feeling?"

My head is still pounding, but instead of answering him, I scramble out of view, sitting up on my knees, checking to make sure that I'm decent. Whoever put me up here has changed me into a man's T-shirt and boxer shorts. If the food weren't tempting me, if my head weren't pounding, if I weren't so confused as to where I am and how I've gotten here, I'd be mortified.

I scoot myself to the edge of the loft and climb down the ladder, which is a piece of art in itself. The rungs are fashioned from actual tree branches, smoothed knots and all. Directly beneath the loft is a galley kitchen decked out in dark mahogany with black marble countertops. The walls themselves look to be made from stacked tree trunks. If I didn't feel like total crap, I'd be marveling over the craftsmanship of this place. "To answer your question, I feel like I was run over by a truck." I blow a curl out of my face.

"I'm not surprised to hear that, but I am sorry. I recommend you rest as much as you can today and drink a lot of water. May I?" He reaches toward my forehead and I nod. His hand is cool and feels good resting there.

"No fever," he announces. "Time to take your mind off things and eat up."

Dominic places the tray on the counter that separates the kitchen from the living space, then pulls out a stool. He arranges the plate and a cup of orange juice before opening drawers and getting napkins and cutlery. With all his fussing, he does a good job of avoiding my gaze.

"Have a seat." He juts his chin toward the counter.

Sitting down on the stool, I breathe in the scents of food. He hands me a fork, knife, and napkin. I place the last on my lap.

"Where am I?" I ask again, fork poised above what looks like an egg scramble.

"You're on our property, in one of our tiny homes."

"Tiny homes?"

The smile he produces warms my fluttering chest and dulls the pain in my temples. I'm not sure I've ever seen him really smile before. Not at me, surely. "When Sheldon asked us to move here, he offered us this place."

"You all live in this teeny house?" There is barely enough room here for two people. How can all four of them live here?

"No." His lips curve. "There are five of these on the property. This one is mine."

"Five little houses? Where? Are we still in the Edge?" I peer out of a window to my right but all I can see are trees.

"Yes, they're called tiny homes. They're ideal for us. We call our community the Grove. I'll give you a tour after breakfast."

"So you each live in one? Not together, but alone?"

He nods.

"But why tiny houses? Why not one large house for all of you?"

Dominic takes in a long breath, holding it for a beat before letting it out. "Our childhood was difficult, unconventional. None of us had our own space, ever. This way we each get a place to call our own and we get to keep it in whatever state works for us. Thorn, for example, is not the cleanest of the bunch so he can keep his place messy. Whereas that would drive me and Rhys insane and we'd be on him all the time."

"Why not just live apart then, in your own apartments or houses?"

"We couldn't bear to be apart from one another. It's a long story. The four of us suffered together and it bonded us, deeply."

"And all of these little houses are next to one another here?"

"Eat your breakfast and then I'll show you." He perches on the stool next to me, jutting his chin toward my plate.

He doesn't have to tell me again, the food is so tempting. Plus I like the way he speaks to me, taking the time to enunciate each word. Besides, maybe he's got a point. I'm brimming with questions, but I'm weak with hunger and not ready for answers just yet. Wrapping myself in Dominic's calm, unhurried presence, I tell myself the world can wait.

Dominic

*S*he falls on the meal like a feral cat that hasn't eaten in weeks. "Delicious," she groans around the food, her cheeks filled like a chipmunk's.

She looks so adorable that I have to stifle a laugh. The last thing I want is to make her uncomfortable or draw her attention to the carefree way she's acting. From what Rhys tells me, this poor girl has never really been free to be herself. Given what I know about this sort of pathology, she may not even know who she truly is. She's lived under the thumb of a dictator her entire life. Her mother would probably be shaming her right now with words like: *We do not talk with our mouths full.* "I'm glad you like it."

"Did you make it?" she asks between bites.

"Thank you, I did. We take turns cooking breakfast. Wait until you taste Thorn's famous pancakes."

"I can't wait. I love pancakes." She pauses, her fork in the air, and beams up at me. Her lovely blue eyes are open and trusting but the trained professional in me can see pain there, too, probably something she'd rather hide.

Her brows furrow a few minutes later. "Can you tell me what happened last night?" Her plate is empty of all but the strip of half-eaten bacon she's toying with, grease dripping down her fingers. Then she freezes, her eyes wide. "Oh, no, I didn't close the show, did I?"

I shake my head, handing her another napkin.

Ignoring it, she asks, "What did they do?"

"It worked out fine. The other performers covered for you. You fainted."

She drops the bacon onto her plate but it bounces off, landing on the floor. "You're kidding, right?" Her mouth gapes open.

"No joke. After your mother's display, you collapsed. But we were all there to help you."

She places her head in her hands, scratching her scalp and rubbing her forehead. The stool wobbles precariously.

"Hey." I reach out to steady her. "Let's move to the couch for a minute."

With glassy eyes, she lets me lead her there. After I make sure she's situated, I get her a glass of water and join her. "Drink this."

Without making eye contact, she does as she's told, handing the glass back to me. She wets her lips. "The last thing I remember is my mother storming out of the dressing room."

"Yes, that's when you fainted."

She gives a little shake of her head, rubbing her forehead again. "I've never fainted in my life. Why?" Her eyes search mine and for once, I can't keep my distance, not when she so obviously needs affection. I put my arm around her, pulling her into me. To my surprise, she nestles against my shoulder without hesitation, wrapping an arm around my middle and sighing.

The smell of her nuzzled up against me is a momentary distraction. And if I had no clue before this moment what my brothers see in this woman, I would get it now. Never before have I met anyone like her. A woman so giving, so emotionally available and strong that it brings out my fierce desire to protect her in every way. Unlike Thorn's cast-offs, a few of whom couldn't seem to stand on their own, I don't mind being her shoulder to cry on. Perhaps because she's too strong to need it. Perhaps because she's not sniffing at me like I'm a runner-up prize.

I clear my throat, bringing my attention back to what *she* wants right now, not what I'm going through from being so close to her. "Sometimes, when a person experiences high emotions like you did last night, their body shuts down. It's a protection mechanism, really. Nothing to worry about or be ashamed of."

"How do you know?" She pulls back to search my face.

"I'm a licensed psychologist. It's also what I do on

the police force. I'm the person who assesses criminals and the like."

She chews her lip absently. "So does that mean there's something wrong with me, psychologically?"

"Not at all." I pat her leg. Shit, bad idea. I snatch it away and focus on her eyes. Not the acres of smooth, creamy skin exposed by the boxer shorts she's wearing. My boxer shorts. Another bad idea. She's not for me, so why is it so satisfying to smother her in my clothes, my scent? "Quite the opposite. Your body knew how to protect itself and reacted accordingly."

"What would have happened if I hadn't fainted?"

I shake my head. "I don't know. Everyone needs an outlet for anger or high emotions. Lashing out is the most common reaction, but everyone is different."

"Lashing out physically?"

"That's one way. Physicality is more frequently a male trait. But people also do it verbally as well. I liken it to a pressure cooker with built-up steam. Where does that steam go? Nowhere until it's let out, given a means of escape. The body is the same way."

"And my means was fainting."

"Exactly. How do you usually blow off steam?"

"Exercise. If I'm upset, I work out. If I'm sad or feeling emotional about something, I spend time with animals, usually my cat or a neighbor's dog."

And if I'm drowning in longing for another man's woman, I would take the first opportunity to lock her in my den. This is exactly what I did. Physician, heal thyself. Yeah, right.

"Dominic?"

"Yeah?" Our gazes lock, her hungry eyes roving across my face. She wolfed down her breakfast already, though I'm not sure that's the kind of meal she's hungry for right now. She throws her arms around me, pressing her lithe body into mine.

"Thank you," she whispers into my ear, nuzzling my neck with her nose.

I give up trying to hide my arousal and pull her closer to me, her body yielding. I'm moving her on top of my throbbing dick when the front door of the little house flies open.

CHAPTER EIGHTEEN

DOMINIC

"*O*h. Um." Rhys stands immobile in the doorway. Iphi nearly falls trying to dismount while I look around for something, anything, to cover my hard-on.

Rhys doesn't move. The four of us haven't had reason to knock before, having lived together for decades with no distinction of mine and yours. The blurred lines of privacy obviously need to be addressed and revised. He's gaping at us, but a smile plays at the corner of his lips.

"Rhys." Iphi rights herself, raising her chin, but the cute flush of red all the way to the tips of her ears gives her away.

"I can come back later." Rhys grins. Wait, grins? Is the man high? Does he not comprehend what a disaster this almost was? "I'm happy to see you're getting to know each other so well." He winks at me. The fucking lunatic. And that's my professional opinion.

"No, no. Stay." Iphi climbs back onto the barstool and resumes eating her breakfast. "Dom was just helping me understand a few things."

Rhys raises his brows.

"About last night," she blurts out. "Not about . . ." She waves a hand around. "Oh, never mind. Just stay. Please."

"Okay." He shrugs, closes the front door, and takes a seat next to her at the counter. "Well I'm glad to see that you're feeling better."

Instead of looking at him or responding, she chugs her remaining orange juice. Even nervous looks good on her.

Time to throw her—and myself—a conversational lifeline. "Rhys lives here, too, you know."

"You do?" she asks. She puts down her empty glass, now on safer ground.

Rhys inclines his head. "I do."

"Why? How?"

He exchanges a look with me, his jaw tightening, then turns back to Iphi. "We're all working on this rogue vampire thing together and I didn't have a place to call home when I got to the Edge. I was in a hotel."

"What about with Chrys, Carter, and Julian?" she asks.

"I didn't want to take Alistair's room. Most of his things were still there when I arrived and it didn't feel right to move them out."

"Plus we had plenty of room here." But in truth there is no way we would have let Rhys stay in a hotel or with his grandfather. Not after Carter's mother all but abandoned him and Nolan when their mother died. After spending basically our entire childhood growing up together, he is undeniably one of us. As crucial to all of us as an arm or a leg.

"Were you all friends growing up?"

"Yeah." That's one word for it. "We've always been tight. We even work together, when we can. Back in NYC, we got Rhys a job teaching martial arts at the police academy we attended, and we're trying to talk Sheldon into adding some continuing education classes for the Edge PD."

"Speaking of teaching," Rhys looks at Iphi, "I'd like to train you. That way you'll be able to defend yourself if one of us isn't around."

"That's a great idea." I pick up the piece of bacon she dropped earlier, toss it in the trash, and then take the seat on the other side of her.

"I'd like that," she agrees. "The independent part

of me definitely wants to learn some self-defense so I don't have to rely on my silver-pepper spray and amulet."

"Great. I'd say we can start after breakfast, but we need your help with something else first." Rhys looks at me.

Shit, how could I have forgotten? It was my idea not to upset Iphi after her fainting spell, but now it's gone on too long without us telling her. Even though it really did slip my mind, with her as a distraction, I know she won't see it that way.

"My help? With what?"

"Iphi." I hold my hands out. "I should have told you sooner and I apologize. I didn't want to upset you before explaining why you fainted and helping you through that."

Her face pales.

"It's Thorn." I wince.

She leaps off her stool, breakfast forgotten. "What's wrong with him?"

I put a hand on her shoulder, resting it there. "Your mother's spell. It's frozen him in his shift."

"He can't change back," adds Rhys.

She rushes to the door. "Why did you guys wait so long to tell me? Male pride? Take me to him. Now."

Iphigenia

The men quickly escort me outside. At any other time, I'd marvel at their unique setup. Tiny homes circle the perimeter, each one cuter than the next. One looks like a white colonial with a tiny bleached porch and ivory columns in the front while two more are distinctly modern in design. The first is painted gray, two large rectangles on either side of slatted wood with floor-to-ceiling elongated windows. The other is smaller and incorporates blond wood with white walls and black trim. And then there's the cutest little hobbit house that almost makes me squeal, complete with a large red round front door. I wonder whose is whose? The one we emerge from looks like a miniature log cabin.

We head toward the blond modern house and up onto its tiny front porch. Dominic knocks and announces us, and Caspian's voice invites us in. I'm surprised this is Caspian's, I'd predicted his would be the hobbit house. When I step inside, he throws his arms around me in a tight hug.

"I was worried about you," he breathes into my hair, tickling my ear.

Pulling back, I beam up at him. His damp, sky-blue eyes blink rapidly. "Thank you, sweetie, I'm fine." I squeeze his hand for good measure and step back to take the place in.

The inside of this house is just as cute as the interior of the previous one, though the wood here is a brassier blond. The ceilings are even higher, glass skylights lining one side of the peaked roof.

A living room and kitchenette are snuggled under two lofts, one in the front and the other in the back. Caspian motions us into the living room, where Thorn, in his mini-dragon shift, is perched on an ottoman.

Running over to him, I hold out both of my hands and he leaps into them. I bring his lizard face up to my mouth and peck the side of it.

Mother has done many despicable things in the past. When Sadie and I were young, she turned my sister into a mouse but didn't tell me or Chrys. When Army had her trapped in my bedroom, I saved her, thinking I was just rescuing an actual mouse. I shudder to think what would have happened if I hadn't been there, but for years I've told myself that Mother would have swooped in from somewhere if I hadn't.

Growing up, I always made up excuses and stories for Mom. But looking at Thorn and taking into account everything else Aurelia has done over the years, to innocents and family alike, to me, last night . . . My body ices over, and I hold Thorn up to my shoulder. He jumps onto it, freeing my hands, and I rub them together for warmth.

"You need white candles, right?"

I jolt. "What?"

"Candles, you need white ones, yes?" repeats Dominic.

Oh, to reverse the spell on Thorn. *Focus, dummy.* I run a hand over his leathery tail in silent apology. "Four white candles and herbs or gemstones. Do you have those?"

"We have a lot of cooking herbs." Caspian opens a cupboard. "Do you want to take a look?"

I walk over with Thorn on my shoulder, realizing that I shouldn't get too excited about this adorable creature perched there, but he's so freaking cool. It would be much cooler though if he weren't *stuck* in this form. How horrible for him, not to be able to change if he wants to. I despise my mother's petty anger all over again.

Peering into the cabinet, I move the jars around but there's not much I can use. "Anything growing outside? A garden, perhaps?"

"We have a small vegetable garden, but no herbs," says Rhys.

"I'm not even sure where to start," I admit. "I have no idea what spell my mother cast. I thought it was a simple freezing spell, but obviously it wasn't, and I don't want to chance making his situation worse."

Thorn nuzzles my ear and I return the caress.

"Is there any hope?" Rhys asks.

"I can go to Sadie's and check her grimoire. I don't think it's a good idea for me to go back to my mother's and look at hers right now."

"Definitely not," agrees Caspian.

"I know we'll need burdock root, that's the main herb used for reversal spells. Can I give one of you a list?"

Rhys reaches out and takes my hand. "Of course. But can't you text your sister, ask her to bring supplies so you don't have to be out of our sight?"

Aw, my knights. "I need to comb through the book first, and it would be better to talk to her in person and see if she has any other ideas. Sadie is more powerful than my mother. I'm sure she can help."

"We'll all go with you to her house then." Dominic takes a step forward.

I take a step back. I'm used to fly-on-the-wall, stoic Dominic. This fierce protector is . . . new. "Don't you guys have to work today?"

Caspian and Dominic exchange looks. "Yeah, but

we'll call in a family emergency," says Dominic, and Caspian nods.

"But I'm not your family."

"Of course you are." Caspian takes a step forward. "And this really is about Thorn, who most definitely is a blood relative. You two are far more important than work."

"I appreciate the offer but that's just too many cooks in the kitchen. Rhys and I will take Thorn to Sadie's."

Caspian and Dominic both posture, arms on hips.

"We want to be there for you," says Dominic.

"For moral support," Caspian adds.

"Sorry, boys, but I've got this."

Caspian growls.

So much for being the calm, sensitive one.

CHAPTER NINETEEN

THORN

*T*he sun is hanging low in the sky when Rhys pulls up to Sadie's house, a small beach cottage with a wide porch sagging under a mountain of potted plants.

I'm glad for the distraction after my brothers' pissing match. I've never seen Caspian that aggro before and no one had any time to talk him off the ledge. I only hope he doesn't strangle Dominic while we're gone. I suspect something may have transpired between Iphi and Dom when Cas wasn't around. Not that I care about any of that drama right now, being stuck as a mini dragon. If it weren't for Iphi, I'd have torched her mother by now. What an evil witch that woman is. I'm unsure what to expect upon meeting one of the girl's sisters. What if they're like her mother? Then again, where did Iphi come from?

A stacked redhead opens the door before anyone rings.

"Well done, sis." Iphi waves toward the lush potted ferns and climbing red vines.

A smile lights up her pale face but those other-worldly green eyes widen when she spots me perched on her sister's shoulder. "I'm crazy jealous that you have a pet dragon."

She did *not* just say that. Curls of smoke puff out of my nostrils in response and I'm mighty close to flaming off her perfectly plucked eyebrows.

"Sadie," Iphi chides. "He's a shifter, not a pet!"

"Er, oops. Sorry. Introduce us?"

Iphi introduces her sister to me, then Rhys, and she sizes him up, tossing her flaming-red waves over a shoulder and holding out a hand.

"Welcome." She flashes a smile that says "do me" and motions for us to enter. I wonder if she and the handsy brunette at Promise are friends.

I hop off Iphi's shoulder and circle the room once, stretching my wings. Her mouth is a tight line and her eyes are narrowed in her sister's direction, but she doesn't say a word. I've heard the rumors about Sadie. She's a sesso, a witch who needs sex in order to use her powers. Sounds like fun to me but I can see how it could become a curse, too. Puberty in the Holt household must have been a trip. Damn Aurelia all over again because I can't tell Iphi how very *not* interested in Sadie I am.

The woman leads us over to two tufted velvet couches straddling a glass coffee table between them. She motions for us all to sit and I perch again on Iphi's shoulder. The living room is a mixture of chrome furniture, lush fabrics, and a jungle's worth of potted plants on the floors, hanging from the ceiling and resting on side tables.

A large book with ancient writing is open on the table. This must be the grimoire Iphi mentioned. I've never seen one before. I want to get closer, but accidentally singeing any of its pages would be a really bad idea. Though I'm still thinking about her eyebrows . . . Next to it sits white candles, a thin dagger that I assume is an athame, and several glass bottles of herbs.

Sadie looks at me and pats the table. The last thing I want to do is leave my woman's shoulder but this is why we're here. The thought of holding Iphigenia in my human form once again blots out my trepidation. I hop off her shoulder and onto the table, next to the book, without turning my head to look at it.

"I'm sorry our mother did this to you," Sadie says

to me and I bow my head. "I've looked through all the spells here, and I'll be honest, I don't know if we can change you back."

A puff of fire escapes before I can stop it, and I'm thankful to be facing away from that ancient book. The fireball hits the corner of the couch and singes a throw pillow. Everyone except for Iphi jumps away.

She leans forward, cooing, "It's going to be okay; we'll figure this out. I won't give up," and rubs the top of my head. She turns to Sadie, who is standing several feet away with her arms crossed underneath her breasts. Even now, she's pushing them up and out. I guess that's what it means to be a sex witch; you have little control over your sexuality. "Why don't you think he can be changed back?"

Sadie returns to the table slowly. "Because our mother doesn't use spells that have been handed down from generation to generation and written in books, especially when she's angry. And, Thorn, do you think you could put a kibosh on the fire-breather act in my house? I'm quite attached to my stuff."

I puff smoke from my nostrils in agreement and she mouths a thank-you.

"Wait a minute, I do not understand what you're saying." Iphi's eyes are moist and her voice has risen an octave.

"Aurelia is like a seasoned chef who's had over a hundred years to practice. She doesn't need a cookbook," Sadie explains.

"Meaning she just makes it up and hopes she gets it right?" asks Rhys.

"Exactly. But I'll give it my best shot. Rhys, you wait over there." Sadie points to the glass patio door. "And, Thorn, either jump on the couch or to the floor. I don't want to break another coffee table if this works."

I jump onto the floor and wait.

Iphi helps her sister position and light the candles in four different directions and one on the coffee table. They do some type of ritual, turning in a circle and drawing something in the air with Sadie's athame.

Once they're done, Iphi and Sadie remain close to me and Rhys stands by the sliding glass doors that lead out to yet more greenery.

Sadie adds dashes of herbs to the candle flame on the table and recites words in another language, one that sounds like Latin. I wait as Iphi glances at me every few seconds. After minutes stretch into an hour, nothing happens.

"Shit, this isn't working," Sadie finally says.

"Maybe if we get Chrys, too?" Iphi wipes at her face with the back of her hand.

She shakes her head. "It's not the amount of power, it's not knowing the correct antidote."

"Maybe another witch's grimoire? Like Katharine's?"

"I already called her. She doesn't have a spell for this either. It would be one thing if Aurelia had changed him into a dragon, but freezing him in a shift . . ." She shakes her head. "I'm sorry, Iphi, but I don't think I can help. Aurelia's going to have to remove this one herself."

"Fat chance of that happening," Iphi sighs. "I left."

Sadie does a double take. "Left as in left home?"

Iphi nods, biting her lip.

"What made you do that? No, wait," Sadie holds up a hand, "don't tell me. I'll guess."

She eyes Iphi up and down but the woman remains still, her hands folded over her chest.

"You finally started to spread your wings, didn't you?" Sadie's lips curve. "Does this have to do with Mr. Hottie Pants?" She inclines her head toward Rhys, who is staring out at the lovely back garden. If he heard her, he's polite enough to ignore it.

But I heard and have to clamp my mouth shut in order to keep the flames in my throat.

Instead of answering, Iphi drops her head and presses her mouth together, looking down her nose at her sister.

"Oh, yes." Sadie rubs her hands together. "Scandalizing. Finally, our younger sister's had enough of the old ball and chain."

"Not nice!" Iphi cries out.

"Well neither is she, Iphs. Time to call a spade a spade. Do you need a place to stay? You're always welcome here but there's more room at Burgundy's. I know she'd love to have you."

"She stays with us," Rhys calls from across the room. Guess he was listening after all.

"Well that sounds fun. You're living with four hot men now." Sadie winks at Iphi. "When you go, you go big, just like me. I approve."

"It's not about going big or trying to hurt Mom or making a point. It was a misunderstanding, that's all. Mom was just reacting in the moment. I'm sure it'll clear up."

Sadie leans close to her sister and drops her voice. "I've always suspected there's more to your powers than you let on. Maybe you're an emotional weathering vane and there's something about Mom that you can sense. Something the rest of us can't? You're an empath, aren't you?"

Iphi's face flushes but she looks away without speaking. Is this true? Can she actually feel what others feel? I'm not sure if that would be a gift or a hindrance.

"Why else would you constantly make excuses for her?" Sadie asks. "Do you really believe that whatever Aurelia's reaction was it was just a misunderstanding?"

Iphi shakes her head, sucking in the inside of her cheek.

"Good. Then here's the clincher." Sadie stands directly in front of her sister, looking down at her. "Do you have any desire to keep living with our mother?"

Iphi's eyes grow moist but she shakes it once, then looks away.

Sadie tilts her own in understanding. Then she recites the words to open the circle and blows out the candles.

Iphi flops on the couch and puts her head in her hands.

No wonder the woman is distraught. She's left the only home she's ever known without making a plan to do so first. Iphigenia, the girl who choreographs every moment of her life. And now she's performing without a net.

Rhys, also seeing Iphi's pain, sits next to her on the couch, weaving his arm around her shoulders. She leans into him, biting her lip. I jump on her lap and push my head into her hand, wishing there was more I could do for her.

"Okay, it's official," says Sadie, "I'm jealous."

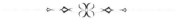

Iphigenia

*B*ack in the car, Thorn sits in my lap, nudging my hand, and I absently pet him.

Rhys starts the car and we move slowly down the drive. I'm so lost in thought that I don't notice where he's driving until we pull up in front of my mother's house.

"Rhys?" Sheer panic is setting in. My hands are clammy and my throat is dry. Swallowing proves to be an effort.

"It's not fair for Thorn to . . ." He cuts the engine, gesturing toward his friend, who is curled up in my lap, sleeping.

He's right, of course. I have to try. Mother may not be happy to see me and I'm not sure what I can say to make her change Thorn back. Maybe nothing. And then what? Guilt for his state flushes through me. There has to be something that my sisters and I can do. If I can at least get Mother to tell me what spell she used, maybe I can reverse-engineer something without her help. Maybe Sadie is wrong. "I'm nervous," I confess, wiping my hands on my jeans.

"I'll go with you."

"It'll be worse if I don't go in alone."

He gets out of the car and comes around to open the passenger door for me, holding out his hand. "With Thorn, then."

Thorn wakes up, stretches, and squawks. Then he flies up to perch on my shoulder.

"With Thorn," I agree. I get out of the car, careful not to dislodge my passenger. I turn toward the house, but Rhys stops me with a touch on my arm. When I turn back, he kisses me, his hands on my arms, pulling me close. Between Thorn's presence and Mother's house looming behind me, I have to pull away before the kiss can deepen as much as I want it to.

"I'll be right outside if you need me."

Steeling myself for the confrontation ahead, I slip my key into the lock, but when I turn it, nothing happens. No click. The lock stays in place. Straightening, I ring the bell *to my own house*. A theatrical gong reminiscent of a French horn rings long and loud. Mother is apparently in no hurry to welcome me home because it's minutes before the handle jiggles and the locks slide open.

"You changed your mind?" Her voice is soggy and

small. She sniffles, holding my gaze, and then spots Thorn on my shoulder. Her hand shoots up. "No, you want your mother to suffer."

I pull my brows together, the pain she's experiencing draping over me like a parachute. "Of course not. Please, I—"

"Please, nothing. You're only here because you want me to change your creature back."

I nod and hold my head up. "Please, Mother. He was only trying to help me."

She narrows her eyes at me and then at the dragon on my shoulder. Her anger slams into me harder than when the ground rushed up to meet my fall after the Trackers cut my silks last year. "It seems that he makes a better pet. A watchdog that can go everywhere with you and protect you. Why on earth should I change him back?"

"Mother," I clench my teeth, "he's a police officer."

"So?" She snorts. "If he had been doing his job, he wouldn't have been sniffing around my daughter."

"Mother, please. This isn't about me."

"Yes, it is, Iphigenia. *You*," she points at me, "made the decision to abandon me. All by yourself. Now you get to live with the consequences, just like I do." I've felt this level of anger from her before but it was never directed at me. My throat tightens and I blink back tears.

Thorn leaps off my shoulder, facing her, flapping his wings between us.

"Your little pet is pushing his luck." As soon as he opens his mouth to spit fire, she slams the door. In my face.

I stand there, looking at the door, biting my lip, and blinking over and over, trying to get my emotions under control.

Thorn squawks loudly, flying back to my shoulder, and Rhys's arms snake around my waist.

"I'm here, baby," he whispers in my ear and I lean back into him, letting him support my weight. With a whoosh, Aurelia's emotions leave me and for the first time in my life, they're replaced by calm. Serenity. The buzzed oblivion I usually only reach a hundred feet in the air before a big crowd.

I look up at Rhys and he smiles down at me, his dark eyes filled with admiration, though the Goddess knows why.

We turn around to walk back to the car when my mother opens the front door again. I spin toward her, beaming. She's had a change of mind after all!

"You'll probably need this when you move in with your new harem." She throws my light-blue valise out of the house, aiming for the grass at least, where it lands with a thud. Her anger is obvious, even without my ability, but for the first time I can't feel her. She's feet away and seething *at me* but there's nothing. Have I gone numb? But no, Rhys and Thorn are bundles of righteous anger at my side, though they, too, feel muted. Like something thick, heavy, and warm has draped my senses from head to foot.

Rhys steps in front of me and Thorn spits a stream of fire from my shoulder, singeing a lock of Aurelia's hair. She yelps, grabbing at the tress.

"This is no way to treat your daughter," Rhys growls. "She's done nothing but put you first, even before herself."

"Your men talk for you, too, now? Fight your battles, with your own mother?"

"My men," I touch Rhys's shoulder, and he steps to the side, still half blocking me, "care more about my well-being than you do. They also see me for who I truly am, not as some extension of themselves or who they want me to be. All I've ever wanted was for my sacrifices to be acknowledged. I didn't even need you to praise me but really, Mom, are you truly incapable of being happy for your daughters when they find their own happiness?"

"If this is your definition of happiness," she motions to Rhys and Thorn, "then no, I can't understand or support it." She slams the door again and I freeze, waiting for the pain to roil through me. But it doesn't.

I take a deep breath, expelling it slowly, and blink my eyes to hold back the tears. They leak out anyway, hot and salty, staining my cheeks. But it's not the messy cry of someone who wants their life back. Nor is it Aurelia's reflected anger. My tears are hot with *my* anger, with determination. I'm crying for my mother, not for myself. And not for the emotions that usually pour from her, no, not this time. This time I'm crying for the mother that my sisters have always known, the one I made excuses for all of my life. The one who can't be happy for her own daughters.

Thorn flies off my shoulder, hovering in the air, and short, angry bursts of fire shoot from his mouth. The flames rival the burnt orange of a violent sunset.

Rhys's big arms wrap me up, turning me, and holding me close as he pets my hair. "I've got you," he breathes into my hair, so strong and sure. And he does. They both do. The strength I need to move past this.

I shudder despite the warm breeze blowing in off the ocean. I lean into him but the tears have stopped flowing.

When someone is put on a pedestal, there's only

one way to go. This is what I get for giving my mother everything. For remaining home when everyone else left. For staying single and being the good daughter. I lost myself for her and it still wasn't enough. It never would have been either. Mother has proven over and over again that when her daughters get their own lives, she washes her hands of them.

So be it.

I wrap my arms around Rhys and pull him in. For a real kiss. The one before was so quick it merely counts as a warm up. This one is all my choice. I'm making the move, here, in front of my mother's house. In front of Thorn. No longer caring what they think. Everything I've experienced before that moment with him is lost in the wind. It whips my hair and pushes my body closer. His hands clutch at my back, his lips warm and wet. My mouth opens for his, my brain no longer in charge. His tongue darts out to explore me and I taste cloves, cardamom. Secrets. The forbidden apple.

"Iphi," he growls into my mouth.

I run my tongue along a sharp fang and cry out when it nicks me.

Pulling away, he holds my face in both his hands. "I'm sorry, did I hurt you?"

"Drink," I moan. "Here. Now. Please." I want him to take me in front of my mother's house. *You think*

I'm a slut, Mama? You think I'm depraved? I'll show you depraved. How about an inter-species orgy on the front lawn?

"No, not like this," he says, those liquid-brown eyes, melting and swirling before me.

"You don't want me?" I cry out, tossing my head to loosen his grip.

"Of course I want you." He cups my chin, lifting my head. He leans down, dusting my lips with his. "But not right here or right now."

He looks toward the house, and I follow his gaze. The drapes are swaying, the house dark. She was watching. Good. For the first time in my life, I feel strong. Not physically. I've been physically strong for years. No, this is a different kind of strength. The kind I always admired in Sadie and Burgundy. A strength of character. A backbone.

Rhys bends down to collect my case and guides me to the car, holding my elbow. I let him. He escorts me in first, then lays my case carefully in the trunk.

Leaning back against the upholstery, I close my eyes. When I open them again, we're back at the Grove.

"Is she okay?" Caspian's voice sounds like he's underwater. The car door opens, and someone touches my face, running their hand down one side and cradling my head. It lolls but I strain to find Rhys and meet Caspian's gentle gaze instead. Does Rhys care that Caspian is touching me like this? Do I? *Stop worrying about everyone else all the time, Iphigenia.* These men can take care of themselves. Before I can say anything, my teeth start chattering. So cold. Numb. The edge of my vision darkens and I strain to stay conscious. Someone unhooks my seat belt and gathers me in their arms. Thorn hovers next to us, a blur.

I'm barely aware of being lifted and carried into a house.

"Don't leave me alone," I breathe into a man's shoulder.

"We're not going anywhere."

CHAPTER TWENTY

IPHIGENIA

*T*he next morning I wake up in the loft bed with two men and a dragon. On one side of me is Caspian and on the other side is Rhys. They're both wrapped around me almost as tightly as my silks.

Thorn is curled up at the top of my head. He wriggles in his sleep and a toasty puff of white smoke hits my face.

All the contact and connection warms my heart. I'm wanted here.

The door to the house opens and the smells of breakfast waft upstairs. Clanking dishes and pantry noises carry into the loft but the men around me are sleeping so I force myself to lie still.

Several minutes later, Dominic's head peeks over

the loft rail and his eyes go wide. His nostrils flare. Then our gazes lock and his eyes narrow on me.

Heat rushes to my face and I writhe, trying to toss the men's bodies off my form.

"Hey, stop spazzing," says Rhys sleepily.

"Get off, Dominic is here," I hiss.

Dom shakes his head, disappointment flashing in those teal eyes.

"So what," Caspian moans.

Thorn jostles above my head, stands up, and stretches out his wings, then crawls toward Dominic.

"I'm going to take Thorn out to relieve himself. Looks like three's a crowd right now anyway." Dom holds out his hand, Thorn jumps on it, and they climb back down the ladder.

"It's not what you think," I gasp, my voice coming out strangled.

The snick of the front door closing is my only answer.

The men shift on either side of me, their eyes opening.

"Was that Dominic?" asks Rhys.

"Yup," says Caspian.

I stretch and shake my head. "I think he hates me." I realize what I've just said a beat too late. No doubt my pink face gives me away.

Caspian chuckles. "No, he probably just wishes he was up here with us." His eyes blink open and his lips brush my flushed cheek.

"Or instead of us." Rhys's fingers snake out to stroke my stomach in lazy circles. The affect is anything but. Little tendrils of flame trail in their wake.

I suck in some air and hold it in my lungs. I don't want him to stop but I'm feeling hesitant, too, with Caspian there and the way Dom reacted.

Caspian leans over me, holding my gaze. Our eyes lock. "Is that all right?" he asks, tilting his head toward Rhys's hand.

I bite my lip and nod. Okay, wow, apparently Caspian has zero issues with this.

"Do you want more?" His voice is so quiet I can barely hear him. He touches the side of my face, his fingers skimming over my cheeks, then into my hair.

"Yes, please." I have no idea what I've just agreed to but having both of them focus on me at once is a fantasy come true. One I didn't even know I had before now, yet the mere idea of it sends little tingles down my spine.

Rhys's fingers trip higher and I suck in another breath, biting back a groan.

"Do you like that?" Caspian growls, hovering

over my face. His eyes are on Rhys's hand and he licks his lips, transferring his gaze to my mouth.

"Yes," I hiss and reach my face toward his.

Caspian leans down to kiss me, taking my mouth hungrily at the same time Rhys's fingers reach my breasts.

Oh, yes. Time to turn off my brain and let these two obviously competent men turn on my body.

Rhys

J pull the covers aside, far enough to expose her beautiful breasts, but conscious of her comfort, I keep a sheet over her lower half. Glancing back up at her, I marvel at the way her loose hair cascades over the pillow. It's exactly the way I like it, unmitigated and free. She's not hiding anything here with us. We've given her a safe place to be who she truly is, without having to wear any of her many disguises.

I slide slower down the bed and straddle her knees, giving Caspian room to work. I trip my fingers over her torso, walking them toward her nipples. Caspian has claimed her mouth and I'm thankful he's distracting her and pleasing her at the same time. Her arching urges me forward and I replace my fingers with my mouth, kissing softly. The woman is purring, which is all the encouragement I need.

I press my mouth to the mounds of her breasts with more force, sucking on her soft skin in little love bites, and move a hand lower, under the covers, to cup her warm pussy. Another moan, but her legs close a little bit. That's all right, I'll wait until she's comfortable. Instead, I reach both hands up to play with her breasts. Pressing her tit into my hand, I knead the tender skin and lick and tease one nipple, then the other. As I pull a nipple into my mouth, she relaxes her legs again and I trail my hand down to her pussy a second time, keeping it over the sheet. This time she lets me, pushing her entire body up and into me, moaning into Caspian's mouth. I peek up, watching their mouths move, the way their tongues are intertwined. Caspian is holding the side of her face with one hand and his other is cradled under her neck.

With Iphi everything is different and I'm still unpacking why exactly. Her naiveté plays a part. Her trust plays a larger one. Her vulnerability transcends both. I couldn't have choreographed this moment any better and it's happening organically. Caspian knows exactly how to transition with me.

Pushing the heel of my palm into her makes her writhe, igniting my own cock. Her skin is burning up through the thin white sheet and I reach down to rub myself with my other hand. All the while I use my mouth to keep working on her tits, longing to suck and bite one of those hard, pink nipples. But I restrain myself. I'm not sure how she'll react to biting; best to keep this round light. I flick a nipple with the tip of my tongue and she groans so I alternate between pressing into her clit and sucking her tit. She's soaked through the sheet, which hardens me even more, my prick throbbing and tensing in my hand. When she writhes and squirms into my hand and my mouth, I bite back a groan of my own. This is exactly what I've been waiting to do to her.

The need to taste her is strong but the last thing I want to do is rush her. Such a strong woman, yet also naive when it comes to sex, that much is obvious. It doesn't mean she's prudish, but it does mean I need to go slow and gentle. No matter how hard I want to take her. I inch my arm up the bed between her body and Caspian's, feeling for my brother's arm, and when I find it he lets me move his hand to her breasts. The man doesn't miss a beat because her breath turns into pants and she writhes even more, bucking her chest and her groin up into both of us.

Though I keep up the palm presses on her clit, I roll to the other side of her to watch her reactions to Caspian. His eyes open and meet mine. I move my gaze to her breasts and smile. Needing no further encouragement, he moves his face down to her tits and commences to lick and suckle her pert nips.

She gurgles with pleasure and throws her head back, elongating that slender neck. Her mouth falls open but her eyes are squeezed shut. She's practically panting with her arms splayed over her head and her thick masses of curls haphazardly spread out around her. The sight of her ecstasy brings my own release close but the last thing I want is to lose my load before we've satiated her.

"Iphi." I move up to her face, softly calling her name, and her eyes slowly open, trying to focus on my face. I lean down to take her mouth, sucking in her lower lip and gently biting it. Her tongue darts between my lips, looking for mine, and when they meet, my heart ignites like a freshly struck match.

Her musky scent grows even through the thin cover, overwhelming in its intoxication. I know Caspian can smell her, too, because he groans. I move my hand to his shoulder, clutching it and pulling him up toward her head. We abandon our tasks at the same moment, him moving from her tits back to her mouth while I move down to her muscular stomach. I peek up and watch him plant light kisses along her cheeks and eyelids. His hand follows along one of her arms until he intertwines his fingers with hers. His eyes flicker open and I shift my gaze to her pussy. He gives me a quick nod, licking his lips and then focuses on her mouth, moving to cover it with his.

Her legs quiver under the sheets, beckoning me, and still I move slowly. I drop kisses on her abdomen and trail my fingers under the covers, tracing the insides of her thighs. She raises her hips up, a clear signal, and I circle her waist with my hands and clutch her close. Pressing my face against her sex through the covers, I breathe her in. Pure ambrosia. I flatten my body on the bed to roll my raging hard-on between my stomach and the mattress.

Iphigenia

*R*hys's face presses hard between my legs, breathing me in and I bite my tongue to keep from yelping.

When the cover disappears over me, I practically leap out of the loft. Then Caspian's tongue pushes between my lips, stilling me. Rhys turns his head to the left and right, growling or maybe humming into my sex. The vibrations carry me further up the steep precipice of arousal.

I turn my head sideways, breaking Caspian's kiss, and try to slide away. "I need a shower," I groan.

"I want you this way, please," Rhys purrs from between my legs, taking another deep breath and holding me still. "You're divine and I need breakfast."

I want to complain, tell him all the reasons why he shouldn't and clamp my legs closed but the sensations rocket through me with such force that my body simmers with overwhelming need. Hot lust courses through my veins and when Caspian covers my mouth again, I open for him, for them both as Rhys moves under the covers. The lion shifter dives in with his velvet tongue and then pulls back out to lick the corners of my mouth, alternating between soft pecks and insistent plunges.

Rhys blows on my heated sex and I squirm.

Holding my thighs in place, he licks my pulsing bud. I've never had oral sex before but I've always wondered and now I know what I've been missing. The one sloppy attempt at intercourse a couple of years ago is wiped from my mind. This is completely different. My heart swells. My heated body tingles and I shiver, pressing my mound up and into Rhys's mouth, where he sucks and licks.

It's like the men know just what I need and I don't have the time right now to unpack the fact that I want them both, equally. And not just in the bedroom, but outside of it, too. And not just them. Why did seeing Dominic so upset affect me as well? Am I falling for him, too, in a different way?

And what about Thorn? Will he be angry that his brothers are here with me, like this, when he's stuck as a dragon? Old programming fills my head—*I'm being insensitive to their needs*. And then I tune into my men. They're lost in this moment of pleasure and both of them want me to enjoy it, too. Caspian, perhaps noticing my distance, pulls back, holding my gaze, willing me back into the moment. There will be time later to sort out the rest.

The pleasure builds again and I let my breath take over, panting strong enough to frost a window. I never thought I could go from zero to sixty in a few seconds but they're proving that I can. Both men follow the crease with their tongues, in unison. Are they mind melding? As if there *were* such a thing. Rhys massages my clit with his soft tongue, alternating between light licks, harder presses, and all-out sucking. He teases me by pressing against the most sensitive part and then pulling away to lick the inside of my thigh. Caspian leans over me to lick my neck and then nibbles down to my breasts.

Pulling Caspian's head down, I arch into him, into both of them. "Harder," I moan and both men bite me gently. "Yes," I cry out.

Caspian squeezes and rolls my nipple between his fingers, little presses that send jolts of heat radiating outward and then shooting down between my legs. Rhys's tongue is hot and firm with its flicking and lapping, first thin and pointed and then flat and wide.

The pressure builds and my body tightens. Rhys stops moving his mouth and presses his hand against my heat. I cry out, begging him not to stop. He shimmies up my body as Caspian sits back to let him and then Rhys takes my mouth while Caspian caresses my body with his hands, tripping ever so softly over my arms. The sensations are strong, and every light touch feels like bellows stoking the flames. My pussy is throbbing and I reach my hand down to touch myself but Caspian stops me, kissing my palms.

"Please," I pant around Rhys's mouth.

Caspian

I lean over her lower body and bury my own face deep in her core. Her thighs are pure muscle and her pussy . . . I've never tasted anything this sweet in my entire life and I want to lap at this woman's essence for all of eternity. I could get drunk on her taste alone. I've been with plenty of other women but no one like this, no one with so much to give that she's forgotten how to receive. *Has she ever received?*

My hands trip featherlight up her taut inner thighs, skimming the surface, barely touching her skin. She bucks fervently into me, crying out for my mouth to take her there.

"Yes, please," she practically shrieks. My cock is throbbing hard, standing at attention under my briefs. But I ignore it, pushing my own wants aside to focus on the needs of our woman. It's about her right now.

I place a finger at her entrance and move it in the tiniest of circles. Iphi cries out, bucking up again. Soon her cries are muffled as Rhys takes her mouth.

I dip one finger inside of her and then pull it back out to skim her clit. She moans into Rhys, making me almost shoot my load into my briefs like a horny teen again.

Her body tenses and Rhys pulls her up and into his embrace. I recognize it as a go-ahead even though we didn't discuss any strategies beforehand. Rhys and I have shared enough women that we can work together without any verbal cues. For Iphi, we can we practically read each other's minds.

I descend on her pussy with my tongue and mouth, ravaging her. The orgasm builds, I can almost follow the flow through her body. The woman bucks madly but we overpower her, holding her down. Her moans and cries urge us on. No time to take care of myself, even though I'm edging and may come everywhere without a single touch.

A growl builds in her throat and then crescendos out as her orgasm bursts through her, long and deep. I wrap my hands around her thighs and hold her body down. Rhys does the same with her torso and arms, both of us pushing down on her while she comes. We look up in unison and smile broadly at each other, then return to watching her come. We cover her body with our hands and mouths while she bucks and writhes like a serpent.

Her eyes snap shut as her body convulses in wave

after wave of pleasure. When she finally stills, we all bask in the glow of the aftermath. Rhys is cradling her in his arms, and I'm stretched out beside her, stroking her powerful legs with one hand. We drift in and out on a blanket of contentment until there's a knock on the door.

CHAPTER TWENTY-ONE

DOMINIC

*T*he minute I enter the Palace, I know exactly what's been going on. It reeks of sex.

Great. I close the door quietly and lean my back against it. Thorn shifts on my shoulder.

My brothers have been enjoying Iphi and I . . . haven't been. I want to be happy for them and for her. Part of me is. The therapist knows this is exactly what she needs, to be worshiped and loved for who she is. To be seen and spoiled. Taken care of in a way she spent her entire life taking care of everyone around her. But what if this girl—*woman*—tears our family apart?

At least she's made her choice now. I wish it was me but maybe Thorn and I can move on, knowing that at least she chose our brothers.

My breakfast sits untouched inside, on the counter, and it's as though I'm standing outside in the cold, shivering. As a tremor passes through my body, Thorn takes flight. I know my reaction is a form of releasing somatic trauma so I can move forward in a healthy way. After I've healed from the loss. At least the worry, jealousy, and pain won't lodge itself in my muscles to cause future post-traumatic stress. But in the moment, it sucks, and I take time to acknowledge the sense of sadness. I step away from the front door and drop my head into my hands.

Thorn flaps noisily in front of me and then flies toward the kitchen counter, landing next to the cold food. He taps his claw against the countertop and tilts his head at me. I sigh and move into the kitchen to make some coffee.

"Dom?" Iphi's sleepy voice drifts down from the loft.

"I'm making coffee," I call back.

"Oh, thank you!" she practically squeals. "I'll be right down." Whispers float by but I clank the coffee pot and cups to give them their privacy.

A moment later, Iphi climbs down dressed in a blue silk robe adorned with silkscreened flowers. I recognize it immediately since I picked it out for her personally and placed it in *her* sleeping loft. My brothers and I decreed that this tiny house should be hers. It matches her personality. The Palace for a radiant queen who possesses our spirits.

Seeing her in the robe melts my heart. The cold I was feeling a few minutes ago disappears completely, replaced by an intense heat.

"You're glowing," I say and reach for her hand. Her cheeks warm to a lovely shade of pink. I turn her hand over and press a kiss into her small palm. Thorn buzzes by my ear and I swat at him before realizing I'm not swatting at an enormous fly.

The dragon tumbles through the air and hits the wall with a thud.

Iphi shrieks and runs to scoop him up, planting kisses all over his body. The guy milks it for everything it's worth, laying prone, and puffing smoke clouds, his eyes closed.

"Dominic, how could you?" she admonishes me.

"It was a total accident, Iph. He's fine. Here, let me see him."

She holds him out to me and I tickle his sides. Thorn writhes and a small flame shoots out of his mouth, then he rights himself and takes off, buzzing around the room.

Iphi giggles, shaking her head.

Caspian and Rhys finally climb out of the loft, wearing self-satisfied grins and partial erections. I snort. Rhys raises his eyebrows at me but Caspian pats me on the shoulder and pads into the kitchen.

"Breakfast looks great, man," he says. "I'm going to reheat it, okay?"

I glare openly at Rhys, and Caspian starts the oven.

"All my men together with me in one place. What more could a girl ask for?" Iphi sits demurely at the counter.

Shit. I'm guilty of doing exactly what I feared would happen between my brothers and myself.

When the coffee is ready, I pour everyone except the dragon a cup and practice every mindfulness technique I can think of to avoid dwelling on painful past events that can't be changed. Remain in the present moment, concentrate on my breathing, and focus on the positive. I pace around the living room, holding a cup of joe in my hands, pausing to look out one of the windows onto our little plot of land.

We've come a long way from the gutters of Manhattan.

"Dom?" Iphi calls to me and I turn away from the window and back to her and the others. She pats the seat next to her and smiles so large that her entire face brightens. Stronger than the morning sun.

Iphigenia

*D*ominic sits next to me at the counter and Rhys on my other side while Caspian removes the plates from the microwave and serves us.

"Thank you for making us breakfast." I look pointedly at Dom and he bobs his head, blinking at me like he's only just noticed something. I try not to be self-conscious even though I want to run into the bathroom and check myself in the mirror. Is there something on my face?

He reaches around me for a pitcher of orange juice and offers me some. Then he tops off our coffee.

My fork is hovering over a mound of delicious-smelling potatoes when Thorn squawks from the couch and flies over to perch on my shoulder. He squawks again when I raise the forkful to my mouth.

"Can he have some?" I ask the men and they shrug.

"He's never had to eat in that form. Usually he changes back," says Dominic.

Thorn emits a low sound into my ear and I hold up a fork of potatoes, which he snarfs down in a messy gulp.

"What are his other two shifts?" I stifle the urge

to slap my palm to my face a split second after the question slips out. It's beyond rude to ask shifters about their shifts. But none of the men seems slighted at my impertinence.

"All dragons. Lucky devil," says Caspian. "Small," he motions toward my shoulder. "Medium, about the size of a bull, and large. What you think of when you think dragon."

"Cool!" I clap my hands together. I can't help thinking that having my very own dragon for a bodyguard is awesome, but my excitement is doused by the surge of his discomfort through my system. What the hell was I thinking?

"I'm sorry, Thorn. I got caught up in the dragon fantasy. That was ridiculously insensitive of me."

I reach up to rub his head, and he pushes into my hand, then nuzzles my neck. A half giggle, half shriek explodes out of me.

"Hey now," says Rhys, looking at Thorn. "None of that at the breakfast bar."

"Yeah, if you don't behave," says Dominic, "we'll cage you."

Thorn widens his mouth and I flinch. Next to my eyes those spiked teeth are quite intimidating.

Even though I know they're joking . . . "No one's caging anyone."

Rhys looks at his watch. "After breakfast, I'd like

to show you some moves before you guys go to work. I can't do it after work since I'm teaching at the vectum tonight." At my confused look, he hastens to explain, "Janice hired me to train some of the girls."

A little knot forms at the base of my throat. I don't want Rhys to teach a class at the vectum. I don't want him to go to the vectum at all. I know what the girls there dress like and how they're encouraged to act. There's even talk that they can be enticed to perform illicit acts for extra money.

"What's wrong?" Rhys peeks at me over a forkful of pancake.

"Nothing," I say quickly.

"It's just work, Iphi. I'm coming home to you."

I toss my head. "You don't owe me anything. You're a free agent." I say the words but I don't believe them, not after our morning together. After the two of them made me come. My entire body flushes with the memory. Still, I want him to want me, not to feel bound to me because of a little sexual play.

"Oh, but I'm not, darling girl. And I can't even put a price on what I owe you."

Although I haven't explored my sexuality as much as most people I know, including my two sisters, there are a lot of things I'm liking so far about this arrangement. I'm glad I've got some open-minded women in my life, Sadie and Burgundy in particular.

"Is everyone working tonight?" I ask, then continue to feed myself and my miniature shoulder warrior.

"We are," the other two men answer. "We've both got the night shift, too," continues Dominic.

"What did Sheldon say about Thorn?"

They exchange looks and Dominic clears his throat. "They're understaffed and he wants him to keep working, says his mini dragon shift could be helpful on the force. After all, that's why Sheldon was willing to take us all at once. But we bought him a little time so he doesn't have to go in quite yet."

"Good." I reach up and scratch under his chin. "I'm not ready to be without him."

After breakfast the men wait outside while I change into a pair of jeans. Even in her anger, Mother did a surprisingly good job packing for me, which says a lot, right? She may be mad now, but the items she included in my suitcase indicate she'll speak to me at some point in the future, unlike the way she treats Chrys. But is that something I want?

Moments later I join the men, who are practicing moves in the grassy area at the center of the Grove. What they're doing looks complicated. Rhys, in his element, is gorgeous. The way he moves, linking one fluid action to the next—he'd fit right in at the circus. I had no idea that self-defense could look so sexy.

"Iphigenia." Rhys stops sparring with Dominic to call me over. "Eventually I'd like to teach you my favorite martial arts forms, push hands in tai chi, but it takes years of practice to be able to thwart an enemy and I'm afraid we don't have that kind of time."

I walk around in a small circle and then hold up my hands in a mock pose. One I've seen in the movies.

He shakes his head but his lips curve up. "You're distracting in an adorable way, but this is serious. We're going to start with basic self-defense moves. In particular, I'm going to teach you some of the moves that were taught to female KGB agents back during the Cold War."

"That sounds scary . . . and cool."

"I'm going to teach you several moves that will either kill your enemy or maim them."

Er, there goes the cool. I cross my arms over my chest. "Uh, no thanks. I'm not interested in killing anyone."

"What if it's kill or be killed?" Dominic asks.

Damn him. "That's too dramatic."

"This is serious, Iphi," Caspian says. "Someone or something is after you."

"You mean Nolan?"

"Where did you hear that name?" says Rhys.

I can't help but take a step back from his menacing tone.

"Iphi, this is important." He takes another step toward me, still wide-eyed and intense.

"Stop!" Miraculously, he does, holding up his hands. "I think it's time to tell me what the hell is going on."

"If we could, we would," says Dominic, "but this is official police business."

Ignoring the shifter, Rhys asks Caspian, "The vampire attacking Iphi, was it Nolan?"

"We've been over this. You saw the sketch yourself," says Caspian after a weighted glance in my direction. "I told you, I'm not sure. his face was deformed."

"Iphi, are you sure? He told you his name? You *talked* to him?" Rhys takes another step toward me, running his fingers through his hair. Something like excitement or hope radiates from him. Caspian flashes him a warning glance.

"I did." I straighten my shoulders. "He didn't want to hurt me. Wait, how do you know his name?"

They all exchange loaded looks. The tension is so thick Thorn could cut through it with his talons.

"We know who he is," says Caspian. "It's why we're all here in the Edge, but that's all we can tell you right now."

I chew on my lip, torn between helping them and helping Nolan. Surely I can do both. Surely they'll react better than Aurelia . . . "Do you know that he's being controlled by someone else? At least, I'm pretty sure he is. He wasn't totally with it."

The men don't say anything for a minute. Despite more glances between them, I can't figure out if they believe me or not. But I hold my ground, tired of explaining myself to people who'd rather stick their heads in the sand than take me seriously. Either they believe me or they don't. Why do they still insist on keeping me in the dark? I'm the one who's not hiding anything. Full disclosure would be nice here. I think I've earned it.

At some unseen signal, Rhys halts further ocular arguments and turns to me. "If you see him again, you need to defend yourself. I'm not saying you should kill him, because I'd rather you didn't. But if you run, he'll catch you. And he could hurt you, maybe in ways your amulet won't protect you against. So let me show you a couple of moves you can use that will incapacitate anyone so you can get away."

I want to ask him who Nolan is but I can tell the conversation is over. And I'm happy to learn what I can do to defend myself without killing anyone. Though I suspect if I had to defend an innocent animal, I'd be more likely to fight.

Several hours later, after both Caspian and Dominic have gone to work, I'm exhausted. Thorn dozes on the grass far enough away that he won't get kicked or stepped on but close enough to watch.

Rhys trained me hard, and I had to compartmentalize, pushing away flashes of his head between my legs. The man focuses on his craft the same way he focuses on my body. All in. He taught me how stomp my foot on top of someone else's foot and break all their bones. He assured me that on a vampire, if I use that move or any of the others he's taught me, they'll heal quickly and it won't permanently disfigure them. Except for the eye gouge, which is only to be used if I'm about to die.

Then it was time to learn the groin grab. At first I thought that would be an easy one. After all, from a young age, we're taught to kick little boys where it counts if they get too aggressive—not that I ever have, mind you. But this move turned out to be different. Rhys instructed me to grab the *testicles*, squeeze, twist, and pull.

"That'll put anyone on the ground for a while," he assured me.

At my gasp, he added, "No, they may not be able to have babies later but would you want a bad guy as a father?"

I shook my head. I've already watched Burgundy struggle with that. But I'm still shaky at the thought of any permanent destruction.

He chuckled. "The groin twist won't kill them, Iph."

Now it's time to practice what I've learned on him. Gulp.

"Try the foot stomp on my foot—just the movement," Rhys says. "Don't use your full strength."

I gear myself up and tap my heel on the top of his booted foot, holding back. After a few times, he removes his boot and places it down in the grass.

"Now full force on the top of the boot."

I thump his shoe but he clucks at me, shaking his head.

"Harder, Iphigenia. Like your life depends on it."

I try over and over again. The last time I practically fall and he has to catch me.

"One more time," he says, righting me.

Shaking my head, I sigh. "I'm tired. Can we go

back inside for a bit?" I hadn't realized how intense Rhys could be in his element.

He checks his watch and nods, then juts his chin back toward the tiny house I've started thinking of as the Palace. "Wait for us inside. I need to talk to Thorn."

CHAPTER TWENTY-TWO

RHYS

When Iphigenia is safely out of earshot, I motion for Thorn to follow me into my house, the Cliff.

The house I've chosen mixes modern architecture with wood and chrome. The hard angles give it the feel of jutting out over a bluff, minus the actual bluff. It's the smaller of the two modern-style homes in the Grove, but the white and blond wood make it appear larger. The palatial wooden porch that juts off one side is the perfect spot to invite everyone over to enjoy our morning coffee.

The wood on the inside is stained gray, making everything clean and expansive. Retreating to the open living room, Thorn perches on my glass coffee table.

"Look, man, I know you're the one who's used to giving orders but at this point you can't so . . ."

He bows his head.

"You'll defer to me for now?"

He huffs smoke from his nostrils, which I take as a yes.

"Good. Well I'm sure I don't need to tell you this but you need to stay with her at all times." He inclines his head. "No bathroom breaks, no food breaks, nothing. Get it?"

He opens his mouth and lets out a tiny stream of fire. I jump back and hold up my hands.

I'm pushing my authority here, but really, what choice do I have? Someone's got to step up and I'm second in command. If Thorn remains a dragon for much longer, we're going to have to figure out a safer way for him to communicate.

"I don't know how long we can hold Sheldon off. He's agreed to grant you a leave of absence but only for a week. I may be able to get him to go for another one, but that'll be pushing it. More likely he'll want you to come in and work cases as a dragon but that will leave Iphi unprotected."

I walk to the kitchen and pour a cup of water, making sure to use glass instead of plastic—images of burnt plastic splattered across his face make me shudder. I place the cup in front of him on the table.

Thorn buries his nose inside the glass, unable to open his mouth, and if the situation weren't so dire, I'd burst out laughing. Pouring him some more water into a glass mixing bowl, I try again and this time he laps at it like a dog.

"Maybe this is a good thing. As a dragon, you'll be able to stay with her at all times and protect her. I think she has the basic moves to defend herself and I'll continue training her, but I don't think she has the heart to actually use them."

Thorn looks up at me, blinking slowly, and the red of his head shimmers, almost like he's going to shift, except he can't.

"She's the reason my brother is even coherent now and he seems to want to fight whatever has a hold on him. Iphi is responsible for all of that. She may very well be his savior."

Thorn flies to my shoulder and I move outside with him to sit on the wide porch in the sunlight for a few minutes.

"All right, let's work together to keep our girl safe."

Thorn jumps down to stretch out on the sun-heated wooden slats. And even though he can't respond, he's a good listener.

"I wish I knew exactly what happened to Nolan. I don't accept that he went mad or chose to be evil.

He's still my brother. Remember how he was angry most of the time we were living on the streets? I think he blamed me for moving us onto the streets with you. He was just too young to understand that Carter's mother didn't want us there."

Thorn tilts his head, planting one of those intense eyes on me.

"And then he just kept pulling farther and farther away, from all of us. But he was never a horrible person. Just confused with unhealed wounds."

Thorn stands and paces along the porch, stretching his wings in the sun.

"I don't know, buddy." I run my fingers through my hair. "He's threatening our woman. I can't help but want to stick close, even though it would appear she's got this."

He opens his mouth as if to add something—more flame, I guess—but closes it instead.

"Thanks for not torching my house." He puffs smoke in reply. If he keeps this up, maybe he can learn to puff rings or something. Morse code. Sign language? Wait, no opposable thumbs, dammit. "Seriously though, man. Iphi. She's a light bearer."

He tilts his head down, agreeing with me.

"If she can save Nolan, well. Then she can do anything."

Thorn hops up on my knee, nodding furiously.

CHAPTER TWENTY-THREE

IPHIGENIA

I miss the guys but I'm glad that Thorn's hanging out with me at the Palace tonight. I make us some dinner and then do my best impression of a slug, lying on the couch and reading a book, waiting for either the guys to return or sleep to claim me. Thorn is curled at my side.

My lazy evening is interrupted when the lights in my house flicker out. I leap off the couch and smack into the coffee table. Thorn lights the room with a tiny stream of fire, which casts long shadows on the walls of the cramped quarters.

Someone is breathing and it's not either one of us.

"Hello?" I back into the nearest wall, and Thorn's head darts left and right, his fire trailing around the room and singeing the walls.

"Thorn, careful," I hiss.

Something drops in the kitchen, and when Thorn turns toward the noise, Nolan appears, holding a large staff. I shiver at the sight. Father carried a staff very much like it for the Scrim before disappearing into another realm.

"Nolan? What are you doing?"

"What needs to be done," says a voice that's not Nolan's, despite coming from his mouth.

Thorn takes to the air, lunging toward him, his mouth open, flames spewing. Nolan slams the staff on the floor once, hard, and Thorn crashes to the floor. A thud reverberates through the tiny home and the lights flicker back on.

I rush to Thorn and scoop up his inert form, pressing my lips to his chest, which still rises and falls. Thankfully, he's not dead. I place him on the couch and turn to face my unwanted guest, firming my stance the way Rhys taught me only a few hours earlier.

Nolan's movements are jerky as he staggers toward me. His eyes are vacant, and judging from the voice, he's being manipulated by the other thing again, the Puppet Master.

"Who are you?"

"Nice try." He lunges for me and I throw down a foot stomp as hard as I can on the top of the vampire's foot. The thing crumbles before me, howling in pain.

I grab Thorn and run to the front door.

"Iphi, wait, please!" a teary Nolan calls out from the floor.

I stop and turn back around. Why do I feel so sorry for him? My empathy is going to be the death of me, but it allows me clarity at moments like this. The Puppet Master has fled, for now.

"Help me," he pleads.

He's like a lost puppy who can't do anything other than his master's bidding, even when he doesn't want to. I can relate. "What can I do? How can I help you?"

"Witch cast a spell?"

I could, but we're talking about an off-the-book spell right now. "Maybe. But why are you turning innocent humans into vampires?" I walk backward to the loft and climb up the ladder with one arm, Thorn under the other. Once I place him on the bed out of harm's way, I back down again.

Nolan gulps air. "Not vampires. Something much, much worse. Master makes me do it. Master wants his army."

"Who is your master, Nolan?"

"Can't say. Can't say. *Can't say!*"

His body twitches and writhes, his head jerking

left, then right. "He won't like it. Won't like. Won't let. Me out."

Rhys

The last thing I wanted was to leave Iphigenia alone at the Grove all night. Thankfully, Thorn is there to watch and help her if needed. And though I doubt she could ever actually hurt anyone using the techniques I've shown her, it still took the edge off my worry and allowed me to focus on teaching.

The girls at the vectum tonight were eager to learn. For this class, I'm focusing on jujitsu, helpful for those who face weaponless opponents, such as vampires.

It's a good crop, ten students with a few martial arts classes under their belts already, all happy to rumble in the garage-turned-gym. Janice has covered it in floor mats and turned it into a teaching arena for her employees, and I've been teaching classes here for a few weeks now. I'm hoping she'll put in a good word for me with Sheldon. After just a few weeks here, the Edge already feels like home, and my cousins agree. Time to put down some roots.

So between Sheldon and Janice, I'm hoping to get the kind of exposure I need to convince a bank to loan me some start-up capital, find a space to rent, and get my dojo going. Even after just a month here, it's clear the Edge has gone through some tough times lately, what with the Trackers stirring up trouble in town last year and a rash of disappearances among the humans the year before that. Sheldon practically hired Dom, Caspian, and Thorn over the phone, the PD is so short on manpower. Sad to say, but this is a town with a lot of demand for self-defense education.

Most of the women in this class are young, in their early twenties. When you're teaching self-defense, women in particular feel vulnerable. They also have to come to terms, psychologically, with the fact that they're being taught how to hurt or kill someone. For many, that's more difficult than learning the moves, and several students are still clearly uncomfortable with the ferocity required, even after three classes.

After the session, I busy myself packing up, eager to get home and make sure Thorn has kept Iphi safe all night. But even though I want to run out the door as soon as class has ended, I stick around in case anyone has an issue they couldn't broach in front of the class.

"Rhys?" Sure enough, one of the younger girls who remained after class to help me clean up has something on her mind.

"Yes, Rose?" Her face flushes a color not dissimilar to her name. Crap. I'm afraid I know exactly what Rose's "issue" is.

"Have y-you . . ." She looks up at the clock mounted on the wall. I follow her gaze. It's late, a little after midnight. "H-have you ever had to hurt someone?"

I stifle a sigh of relief. "I have and you will be able to as well, but hopefully you'll never find yourself in a position where that'll be tested."

She nods and looks away.

I turn back to the closet and finish putting everything away.

"Rhys?"

"Yeah, Rose?"

"Could I get a ride home? I'm not too far from here."

I want to say no so I can return to Iphi sooner, but there is no way I'm letting this girl walk home alone at this time of night, especially since there are baddies running around town.

"Sure, let's go." I wait until she exits and then turn off the lights, lock the door, and follow her to my car, careful to keep some space between us.

I open the passenger door for her and she looks up at me under her lashes as she slides in.

She buckles herself in and then licks her lips. Her perfume, thick and cloying in such a confined space, makes my eyes water.

I roll down my window. "Where do you live?"

"In that orange apartment complex near Plum Street. You know it?"

"I do."

We drive there in silence and a few minutes later I pull up in front of her building.

"Do you mind walking me to the door?" She looks out the window nervously.

I bite my tongue, stuffing down my first response. "Of course." It's not Rose's fault that I'm worried about my own girl and not her.

On autopilot, I exit the car and walk around to open her door. Once outside, she throws her arms around my neck and pushes her body against mine. Her perfume was bad enough in the car; now it's climbing up into my nostrils like kudzu. She turns her face toward mine, heading in for a kiss. I turn aside so she merely swipes my cheek, then wrap my hands around her wrists to open her arms and twist out of her grasp.

"Rose, I'm sorry if I gave you the wrong idea. That wasn't my intention."

The girl lets out a small hiccough, her face crumpling and reddening at the same time. She looks down and kicks at something invisible on the ground. "Well, she's a very lucky girl." She turns, firms her shoulders, and walks toward her house. At her front door, with her back to me, she calls out, "I hope she knows that."

CHAPTER TWENTY-FOUR

IPHIGENIA

*a*fter Nolan has calmed down and returned to a quasi-normal state, I sit him on a chair in the center of the living room. I put all the gathered herbs and implements I can think of for the spell on a side table in front of him. Mother packed my candles and athame. Proof she doesn't hate me?

I don't believe he could or would hurt me, even with his master pulling his strings. But I do know that going behind the men's backs and doing what I think is right could hurt *them* emotionally. I hope that after they see the results, they'll understand. I have to try. Another lost puppy needs my help.

The vampire's eyes grow big. He looks a lot younger than his appearance would suggest. His brown eyes are a shade or two lighter in the dim light and I suddenly have the urge to take him in my arms and promise him that everything will work out.

Instead, I light the four candles in the four directions, drawing the circle and closing it around us. I light another candle in the center, open up a clean piece of cheesecloth, and begin adding pinches of each herb. First I use my favorite protection herbs. Althea for protection from psychic powers. Juniper berries for self-defense and exorcism. Honeysuckle, frankincense, and euphorbia. One pinch of each goes onto the cheesecloth and another into the flame. Throughout the ritual I chant for his protection and freedom from his master's influence. *"Praesidium. Praesidii Nolan. Et psychica de necessitudines Nolana est dominus disrupti sunt."*

When the amulet's contents are assembled, I gather the edges of the cheesecloth, attach some string, and place it around Nolan's neck, continuing to chant throughout. Then I ask him to repeat the words after me before beginning my binding chant.

"Aliquis concutiens ex. For the greater good of all beings, the inhabitants of Distant Edge and Nolan, let this protection spell free him from his master's hold." The protection bundle he wears is knotted and tied so its contents will stay together. With the words focusing my power and its contents focusing my intent, I bind the spell into existence for now and

always. "By the power of three times three, so mote it be."

Nolan's body shakes and convulses in the chair. No wait, it's not Nolan shaking, it's the chair.

"Hold on to the arms, Nolan. Wait it out, don't get up yet."

He's writhing in pain now, too, like he's being shaken by an external force, but he holds on while the chair bucks beneath him.

Once it stops, I blow out the candles, open the circle, and turn on a floor lamp in the living room. The eerie cast to Nolan's face is gone. His scars remain but they've lightened, become less pronounced. Even his hair is different, a thick, lustrous brown, shining with health. If I didn't know this was Nolan, I'd think he was an entirely different person.

"You can't take off the amulet if you want to stay protected. Understand?"

He nods.

"You also have to stop drinking from anyone." I think of my poor neighbor, wasting away after his bite. I can't take the risk that Nolan might be . . . changing humans somehow. Turning them into some sick mockery of vampirism. He's going vegan until I can figure out if he's changing humans because of a spell cast by his master or because there's something wrong with him, some virus or anomaly.

"How am I supposed to eat?"

"We'll figure it out. I know someone at a vectum."

He looks away and offers a small nod.

"Good, then it's understood?"

"Why are you doing this for me? I know you have a huge heart but this . . . This is hard to believe."

"No ulterior motives here." I put my hand on my chest. "My reward is helping someone in need. That's what I do. It's who I am."

"Are you Florence Nightingale or Mother Teresa?"

The snide response irks me. "I just *like* helping others, okay?"

"I'm sorry, Iphigenia. It's just, no one's really helped me before."

I can't help but soften. "Well, someone is now, so please abide by the rules if you want to remain your own free agent. All right?"

"Yes, of course. Will I be able to see my brother soon?"

"Your brother?"

"Rhys."

The room spins for a moment. I'm so lightheaded I have to sit down on the floor. "Rhys? Rhys is your brother?"

"I thought you knew." He approaches me slowly, holding out a hand, but I shake my head and his arm drops to his side.

I want to help him but that doesn't mean I'm comfortable with him touching me, and now with the news that he's Rhys's brother . . . Why didn't anyone tell me? My entire body goes cold. Were they trying to protect me or was it a trust issue?

And who cares? This is not news that should have been withheld. They knew Nolan was interested in me. Did they really think I wouldn't learn of their connection on my own? That it wouldn't hurt me when I did?

"Iphi?"

"I don't know, Nolan. We should probably wait to make sure that you're really free and clear first." But I know he is. His entire appearance has changed, his demeanor, too. Maybe my current motivation to keep him away from his brother is coming from spite. "How many vampires did you make?"

He shakes his head. "Not vampires. That's not what they become. I don't know what they are. But I'm not sure how many. Everyone I drank from turned. *Dozens.*" His healthy skin grows green again. I'd be worried the spell was unraveling, except it's simple horror tinting his skin now.

"And where are they? How come more people don't know about them?"

"A few have stayed in their houses and reported the assaults as animal attacks. Most, though . . . the master takes them for use in his army."

"And where is he located? Does he have a secret lair?" I'm not sure why I pulled that out but with the word "master" one does think of "lair."

"No clue."

He's not lying. "Right then. It's time for you to go so we don't get caught." Famous last words. I help him to his feet just as the front door to Thorn's house slams open. Rhys is home, and he's not happy.

Rhys

*W*ithout a second thought, I pounce, throwing my brother to the floor and holding him there.

"What the fuck are you doing here?" I growl. "Iphi, are you okay?"

"I'm fine. Get off Nolan. Now!"

I chance a look at her, hands perched on her hips. "I'll do no such thing. He's dangerous." Though he's not fighting me—he's completely limp under me on the floor. Because he's already turned her?

"I'm not anymore. Your girlfriend fixed that. She fixed me," Nolan pants, gulping in air.

I ease off his chest. Iphi doesn't look bitten. And Nolan looks fine, not the disfigured wreck in Caspian's drawing. There are a mess of scars he didn't have before though. A lot of them. But he's acting calm. He even makes eye contact with me. It's his eyes that finally let hope seep in—they're clear, direct. Not hiding hunger or madness from me. "Nolan? Is that really you? Did you really break the curse?"

"It wasn't a curse, it was much worse than that. But I'm harmless now. As long as I don't bite anyone."

"Which he's agreed not to." Iphi crosses her arms over her chest and narrows her eyes at me. "Do you want to explain why you failed to mention that he's your brother?"

I flinch. "I—" Shit. I run my fingers through my hair. "Iphi—"

She points to her front door. "Out. Now."

"I'm not leaving you alone with him."

"Fine, then both of you can leave."

I stall. "Where's Thorn?"

Her features soften and she runs to the loft,

climbing up the ladder. A moment later, she leans down to hand me the sleeping dragon but I have to leave Nolan to grab Thorn.

I glare at my brother. "Why isn't he waking up?"

"It's my fault," his eyebrows draw tightly together, "before Iphi helped with the spell she cast. I'm not sure what I did but . . ."

Iphi steps between us, palms out toward me. "He was being controlled. It wasn't his fault."

She's protecting him? So fiercely, after all the havoc he's been wreaking? Just more proof of her ginormous heart. "Can you do anything to help Thorn?"

"I could try."

"It'll wear off in about an hour," says Nolan. "Whenever I use that crazy staff, the spells don't last for long."

"You came in here with a magic staff? To hurt my girl? To make her a *ghoul*?" I growl, taking a step closer even though Iph still stands between us. "And then you hurt Thorn?"

Nolan flinches. I don't know why I'm listening to these lies. My brother already attacked Iphi twice and tried a third time while I wasn't home to protect her. He may have hurt Thorn with some unknown spell.

"Shhh, Rhys, it's okay." Iphi leans in, one hand

going to my chest, her voice calm and coaxing. "I already told you. Nolan came to me for help. He never hurt me. He never even wanted to hurt me. He just needed my help. I'm all right. I was never in any danger. I'm not a g-ghoul."

I know what she's doing, with her low and easy voice, the soothing hand rubbing my chest and arm. I'm not some stray on the side of the road to be lulled by her charms, but damned if isn't working.

As if sensing my panic easing, she leans in farther to wrap her arms around my chest, pulling toward her. She exhales, then cuddles me closer. I lean into her, helpless to resist.

She rubs her face in the crook of my neck. "There, now we can talk like civil—" She stiffens, sniffs, then springs away.

"You asshole! You call me 'darling girl' then come home reeking of another woman's perfume?" Iphi tears open the door and flees into the night, alone.

CHAPTER TWENTY-FIVE

IPHIGENIA

igures. I don't know what I was thinking. He was smothering me in waves of guilt. But was it for me or for her?

There's really no reason Rhys wouldn't be seeing other women. It's not like we ever had a conversation about being exclusive. Plus he shared me with Caspian, so if I were to think he was mine alone, wouldn't I be the hypocritical one?

Then why does it hurt so much? My thoughts are jumbled as I run away from the Grove. I know I should stay and try to talk it out but I'm being led by my emotions and they're winning.

After a few minutes I stop and talk myself down. Rhys hasn't pledged himself to me. I don't own him. Unless I tell him otherwise, isn't he free to do as he pleases? Of course other women find him attractive and of course he'd be interested in pursuing them. After all, in that department, he probably thinks he has to share me. And maybe he does. Again, another conversation we never had. *"There needs to be a lot of open communication and no hidden feelings,"* Burgundy said. Epic fail so far.

The snap of a tree branch sets me on high alert. I freeze, but without the light of the moon, I can't see anything but darkness. The sound of my breathing fills my ears. Forcing myself to stop and listen, my senses heighten. Another snap and then I am flat on my back with a snapping creature at my neck. I'm getting so tired of this position.

I push her away with both hands but I'm no match for her. There's only a split second to wonder why she can even touch me with my amulet on. She hovers above me, jaw opening, head dropping to my neck. I close my eyes, waiting for the sting of the bite, but my amulet finally does its job.

Whoosh, the air stirs around me and I wrench my eyes open. Rhys and Nolan have yanked the vampire off me and tossed her away as though she were made of cardboard. They turn to her with open mouths, their own fangs flashing in the moonlight.

"Wait! It's not her fault. She doesn't know what she's doing."

"She was trying to kill you," Rhys growls.

"Can you restrain her? Bring her to Sheldon so he can run some tests, try and figure out what's going on medically? Magically?"

Nolan grabs her and Rhys shakes his head at me. "Such a big heart." His tone makes it sound like a tragic disease rather than a strength.

I blink up at him. "I can't help it. She's a victim, too."

"This is why I love you." He kisses me deeply but I bite his tongue.

"Ouch." His head snaps back. "What was that for?"

My mind reels with the words he's just spoken, but my flaring anger wins. Is he just trying to distract me from the woman he was with earlier?

"We'll talk about this later," I say through clenched teeth.

"I've got her," Nolan calls out, holding the writhing woman from behind in a headlock.

We walk back to the Grove together, Nolan leading with the female in a choke hold.

"We aren't good?" Rhys reaches for my hand but I pull it away.

"Nope."

When we reach the opening to our residences, Dominic and Caspian are walking toward us.

"I thought you guys were still at work," I say.

"Rhys texted and told us to come home. I'm glad he found you. You had us worried." Caspian hugs me tightly and I throw my arms around him, burying my face in his shoulder. He pets my hair. At least *he* doesn't smell like some floozy's perfume.

"What's this?" Dominic juts his chin toward the female . . . ghoul. A word I'm still trying to assimilate.

"She was trying to attack Iphi. Do you guys have any vampire-proof handcuffs?" Rhys asks.

"In the car," says Dominic. "I'll get 'em." He nods toward Rhys's brother. "Nolan, man, wow, I'm really glad to see you're okay."

Caspian lets me go and eyes Nolan. "What the hell happened to you and how are you basically fine now?"

"For now," says Rhys. "It may not hold."

"Probably best to unload everything later," Nolan says.

"Well it's really good to see you." Caspian claps a hand on Nolan's shoulder and squeezes tight.

Several minutes later, Dominic returns with silver handcuffs and restrains the woman, who is now subdued.

"Where am I?" she asks, looking around. "Why am I handcuffed? Where are you taking me?"

My already bleeding heart opens even more,

gushing now. "I'm sorry. No one's going to hurt you. We're trying to help."

Her head spins toward me. "There's no help for me," she hisses, the syllables low, sibilant, and venomous, and Dominic hauls her away toward his car.

*a*fter Dominic leaves to take the woman to the station, we gather in the Palace again. Thorn's snores waft through from the loft as the men right furniture and I clean up the remnants of my spell casting.

"Why is Thorn sleeping through all of this?" Caspian asks and I explain what happened with the attack, Thorn's attempted defense, and Nolan's staff. "And you wrangled Nolan, too? He was pretty rabid."

"Right here, man," says Nolan and I laugh even though I don't want to.

But Caspian doesn't even crack a grin. "Will the spell on Nolan hold?"

"I don't know," I admit. "And it's not really a spell, it's an amulet, like this one." I hold up my silver pendant. "As long as he has it on, he should be safe, but . . ."

The men exchange looks.

"I don't like it," says Rhys. "I'm grateful that you wanted to help my brother. I'm grateful that you *did* help him, but, Iphi, you put yourself in grave danger to do it, and with Thorn out, there was no one to protect you. You could be dead right now. Or worse."

"Is it so hard to believe that I don't always need protecting?" My voice rises to a high shrill. I know I'm overreacting—because he doesn't know how right he is. I don't think Nolan was sent here to make me a ghoul. But I am *so* not sharing that insight right now because I'd like to see daylight again before my twenty-first birthday. "Even after all this time together, you still don't trust my judgment?"

"This isn't about that," Caspian says. "Rhys is right, you should have waited for us to have your back."

"Rhys is right?" I put my hands on my hips. "The man who spent the night with another woman? I was here alone while you two were out doing who knows what."

Caspian narrows his eyes at Rhys. "Another woman? Why would you do that?"

Rhys lets out an exasperated groan. "I was not with another woman, not in that way. I drove a student home. She needed a ride. When I dropped her off, she threw her arms around me. I set her straight. Nothing happened."

His sincerity is a clear note in my head, ringing so loud it almost hurts. I can actually feel his heart aching for me. My own anger crumbles in its wake. It must have overridden my access earlier, something that hasn't happened for years, not since I realized what my gift was and started honing it. Keeping my own emotions in check before I can access another's isn't usually an issue. But I've been anything but centered since Rhys walked through my door. "I believe you."

"Because of your beautiful trusting nature," Rhys says. "But you can't think with just your emotions, Iphi. That could get you killed."

I'm not mad anymore, but that doesn't mean I can afford to back down. This is too important if we're ever going to work past tonight. "Why are you patronizing me? We love quality A in Iphigenia but quality B has gotta go? I'm an entire package. You've encouraged me to be free, to make my own decisions, and stand on my own two feet. But when I do, according to you two, I've made the wrong ones? I'm strong but not strong enough to survive without you?"

Rhys stops pacing and clamps his mouth shut.

Caspian goes rigid, like I've finally shocked some sense into him.

"I love that you have my back, I want that, but I need this to be a team. I'm not some fragile little doll that needs special handling."

"Of course not," says Caspian. "We don't think you are."

"It's just that if anything had happened to you, we'd blame ourselves." Rhys's dark eyes search mine.

"But our girl took care of herself and tamed the big bad vampire, too," says Caspian, moving behind me. He presses into my back, wrapping his arms around me. I lean into him, softening.

"Hey, guys?" Nolan says. "I love what you've all got going here and I'm not one to judge. Especially after what I've been through, but I feel like a fourth wheel. Is there somewhere else I can crash tonight?"

"Of course, bro." Rhys holds my gaze until I offer him a curt nod. Then he turns to Caspian. "I'll take him to my house for the night. Be right back."

The unsaid words "keep your eye on Iphi" are nonetheless loud and clear, but after all the upheaval, it doesn't annoy me for once. I like having four strong men at my disposal—as long as they respect my ability to take care of myself.

"You tired?" he asks me after Rhys and Nolan leave.

"Yeah, but is this okay?"

"What do you mean 'okay'?"

"Well, isn't what we're doing a bit weird? What happened the other night. It's all beyond normal societal standards."

"Rules are just made-up things, Iphigenia. Someone makes them up and imposes them on others, for good reasons or bad. With enough power behind them, the group goes along with it. Especially if there are consequences for not doing so. Who's to say that the three of us can't make up our own rules? Who will stop us if we do? Are you interested in both of us? In the same way we're interested in you?"

I tilt my head down but look up at him through my lashes, trying to hide the heated flush that rushes to my face. "You know I am."

He takes both of my hands in his. "Then we'll work it out."

I turn my face up and stand on tiptoes but I don't have to say a word. His lips meet mine with an unexpected ferocity. This soft-spoken artist does not hold back. As our tongues meet and dance together, a long sigh escapes my mouth into his. Those firm hands pull me in tighter and just as I start to lose myself in the passion, Thorn emits a loud snore. We can't help but stop and laugh.

Caspian leads me over to the couch. Sinking

down, he pulls me on top of him, and I happily straddle his lap.

"This way you can lead." His voice is thick. "I don't want you to do anything you're not comfortable doing."

Leaning into his mouth, I probe the hard ridge of his lips, licking across the seam until they curve into a smile and then I lick along the edge of that, too. One strong hand holds my back and the other tangles in my hair.

"You taste like starlight," he says and then he takes my mouth, hard like before. Biting and licking, sucking and exploring with an urgent need. Our mouths lock together and my consciousness slips into a deeper state. A state without logic. A state beyond measure. My mind can't grasp what's happening, can't make sense of these men, of this man, so instead I let go, letting my body sink into the fervor. A warm, tingling sensation travels downward, coursing along a hidden pathway through the center of my body and settling between my legs.

I'm barely aware of moving his hands from my back to my breasts. Urging him to clutch me there, my own hands resting on top of his, I show him how to touch me. Squeeze here, pinch there, rub everywhere. The sound of the front door opening and closing doesn't bring me out of our entwined passion. I can't stop. I don't want to stop. I moan into Caspian's mouth, knowing that Rhys is probably watching us.

Caspian's hands cup my breasts, alternately kneading them, and tugging on my nipples. My head flies back but I keep my eyes tightly shut and pull one of my breasts free from my tight camisole so it spills over the rigid underwire. There are two gasps, one from Caspian and the other from Rhys. Confirmed. He *is* watching. Caspian's mouth moves to my chest, taking the freed nipple and licking it, teasing it with just the tip of his tongue. A zing shoots straight down to my core.

"Rhys." I open my eyes, my head still back. He's standing motionless in front of the closed door, his eyes on mine. "Kiss me," I growl, the low murmur pushing out of my throat. Caspian stops tonguing my nipple to look up so I push his head down and he chuckles, cupping me there and taking my entire nipple into his mouth to suck it.

Rhys moves closer, goes down to his knees next to me, and fits his mouth over mine, cradling my head. Caspian pulls my other breast free and moves to suck on that nipple while massaging the other one. Warm, vibrant light courses through my entire body, lighting me up from the inside. Rhys's kiss is completely different from Caspian's. His lips are hot but tender, playful, as he nibbles at my mouth. I pant into him, reaching for his hand, bringing it to the breast Caspian is neglecting. I grind down as Caspian's hardness pushes where I'm straddling him and he groans and bucks up into me. And then I'm being lifted. Rhys and Caspian lay me down lengthwise on the couch. My knees are up and both of my breasts are exposed.

"Is this okay?" asks Caspian.

"Yes, I want this." My voice is barely audible but they hear me, and each one sits next to me on the floor.

I turn my head toward Caspian and his mouth claims me while Rhys drops to my breasts. He sucks and nibbles on my nipples as Caspian winds his tongue around mine.

Both of their hands are on my body, exploring me, stroking my heated skin. A hand brushes over my mound and I widen my legs on a moan. The hand palms my sex, pushing into my clit with the heel. Pleasure rockets upward and I arch my back, bucking into the hand.

With one of my own hands I grab Caspian's hair and drag him onto my lips. With my other, I grab Rhys's hair and push down. He needs no further encouragement before unbuttoning my camisole, following his fingers with kisses. Delicate and gentle, his lips trace the contours of my body. I reach down between Caspian's legs to feel the hardness swollen there but he moves my hand to his chest, breaks the kiss, and whispers in my ear. "Let us take care of you."

"You've been doing that," I groan. "I want to feel you inside me."

He growls.

Leaning my head back, I bite my lower lip, and raise one eyebrow encouragingly.

"Oh, Iphi," he groans, then covers my face with kisses.

Rhys is busy unbuttoning my jeans and tugging them down. I lift my hips to help him. He presses his face into my heat and breathes. "You smell so good, baby. Can you open your legs a little more for me?"

I do as I'm told while Caspian kisses down to my breasts again. I miss the feel of his lips on mine, of one of their lips on mine, but the loss is quickly replaced with the thrumming of Rhys's fingers over my pussy lips. I'm still wearing panties and the way he's touching me is so intense that I can't imagine not having that barrier to stop myself from going over the edge.

His face presses into me there again and he breathes in and nibbles on my lips through the fabric.

"Caspian, man, you've got to smell her." His voice is heavy with lust. "Her scent is even better than last time. I can't keep this to myself."

I expect them to change places or something but Caspian drops to his knees next to me and buries his face where Rhys's was, breathing deeply. He groans and pulls my panties to the side. I look down in concern but both men are on their knees and the look on their faces is one of worship. I've never seen any man look at me like that, let alone my pussy.

Hands move up my thighs and I slide my butt down a little, toward my admirers. A tongue on my labia startles me and I wriggle in place but the soft waves of pleasure that radiate up from my core keep me put. Hands push my thighs open even wider and the men take turns licking me. There are mouths and tongues on my pussy, my inner thighs, and my stomach.

A mouth latches on to my clit and I buck. A finger presses against my entrance and the fervor builds.

"Kiss me," I gurgle and within seconds a mouth is on mine, tasting of me. The other mouth is below, working some incredible magic. I'm flying through the air, tumbling from a massive height, wrapped tightly in my silks. And this time two strong men are waiting there to catch me.

The heat builds, trembling through my body. It intensifies, magnifies, reaches through me, and out of my extremities until pure white light explodes behind my eyelids and the orgasm flows through me like a long, twisting, turning drop down silk strung from the moon itself.

My body bucks, almost leaving the couch, but the man attached to my lips above eases me down. And the man attached to my lips below stills, cupping his warm mouth over my throbbing sex.

"I need to feel you both inside me," I practically scream. "Fill me up." I wiggle my hips, hoping to entice. No more words are needed. Both men fight their way out of their jeans. I watch with a lazy smile.

"Only if you come again for us," Rhys murmers, dropping his boxers. I sit up on my elbows. His dick is long and hard, pulsating for me, the dark hair around it cropped short. He rips a condom wrapper open with his sharp canines and rolls it on while I watch. Who knew that could be so hot?

I open my legs wider and look up at Caspian. He's standing next to me, his dick in hand, little blond wisps of hair curling around the base. Caspian is thicker than Rhys but the sight of both make me twitch with need.

Rhys fits himself between my legs and guides

himself toward my entrance, watching me. My eyes are glued to his but my hands have a mind of their own and reach next to me, wrapping around Caspian's hard cock and pulling him closer.

"Oh, yes, baby." Rhys is all growls now, the words guttural and hard to discern as he guides himself into me.

When his hard cock presses at my entrance, I arch my ass higher and drop my head back.

I grip Caspian's huge cock harder and Rhys guides his own cock into my drenched pussy. There's a moment of intense stretching that morphs into a deep pressure, then overwhelming pleasure.

Caspian gently removes my hand and licks it before returning it to his cock.

Both men fuck me in synch, their rhythm slow and controlled as I get used to them. Caspian pumps into my hand and I reach my other to join it, clenching the base of his cock, and tickling his balls. I don't really know what I'm doing but his groans tell me it's working. He bends forward, his hands moving to my breasts, pinching, tugging, and rolling my nipples.

Rhys's cock fits perfectly, rubbing my clit from the inside out, filling a deep, wanton need. Another orgasm builds.

Hearing both men moan while they fuck me in unison pushes me over.

I roar as the men tease out my climax. A deep heat floods my core, filling every cell, washing me in a golden white light. I buck and shake, my pussy latching on to Rhys, and my hands latching on to Caspian so tightly that both men explode mere seconds after I do.

Rhys thrusts hard into me just as the last of my orgasm hits, and he shouts, grabs my waist, and shoots deep inside of me. His cock pulses, deep inside my canal. Caspian gasps and groans, shooting onto my breasts.

So lost are we in the height of our passion that the sound of a door opening barely registers.

CHAPTER TWENTY-SIX

DOMINIC

*T*he door thunks against my ass. On autopilot, I shuffle forward and pull it shut behind me. I should be leaving, but instead I'm pulled forward. The shock of seeing Iphigenia spread out on the couch with her legs wide and her breasts on view is only slightly more shocking than seeing my brother and cousin clamped together on her body.

I know they share women occasionally, but I've never seen it before. The image is burning itself into my retina, a thousand times worse than anything my imagination supplied before, because they've been enjoying the woman that I want for my own. My psychologist brain kicks in and tells me that our brotherhood far outweighs my own desires. My caveman brain wants to club my psychologist brain until it shuts the hell up.

Her eyes open, glazed and languid, and meet mine. I may be a professional but I have no idea how to react. My body betrays me. This sensual scene is a turn-on, I can't deny it, but lust isn't the only thing I'm feeling. Heat builds in my core, passion mixing with anger.

The look she's giving me may well be a plea for acceptance. The last thing I want to do is shame her, but can't she see that she's being selfish right now? Why isn't she thinking of the big picture or the future? Why isn't she worried about the relationship that we've all striven to create?

Her brows crease like she knows what I'm thinking and I turn away, giving her my back. Hell, maybe she does. Rhys thinks she's an empath, after all. I hope she thinks I'm just giving her some privacy but the truth is it hurts to see her this way, with them.

Shit. I have to be the bigger man here. I have to be happy for my brothers, especially if I want to keep our family together.

"Hey, guys," I say aloud. "Didn't realize what I was walking into."

"No worries, man," Caspian says. "She's decent now."

I turn back around. They've covered her with a blanket from the back of the couch. For this I'm both thankful and annoyed for the same reasons, not having the distraction of her gorgeous body.

She expels a sexy little *mmmmmm* before curling up on the sofa as the men busy themselves getting dressed.

Rhys then climbs into the loft and Caspian shoots me a grin, going into the kitchen to grab some water. I still can't move. My brain wars with my body. A moment later Rhys climbs back down holding a fluffy pink robe in one hand and clutching the sleeping Thorn to his chest with his other hand. He moves to Iphi's side on the couch. Whispering in her ear he places the robe over the blanket and sets Thorn down carefully in front of her. When he's about to pull back Iphi's hand darts out and clutches his wrist. A pang of envy shoots through me. I can't help it. At face value, the tiny movement doesn't seem as intimate as sex but I know it's much more personal. It tells me she trusts him. It tells me they've formed a secure bond. It tells me I'm too late.

I whirl around again, mostly to hide my distress but also to give her the privacy she needs to don the robe.

A moment later Caspian taps me on the shoulder and juts his chin toward the couch. I spin back to the vision of Iph, sitting in the center of the sofa, wrapped in a fluffy pink robe that on anyone else would look matronly. But on her it looks both sexy *and* adorable. Rhys is perched on one side of her and Thorn sleeps in her lap, gently snoring. She's absently resting her hand on his rump. Shit, I'm even jealous of my brother, conked out in his dragon shift right now. This will not do.

Caspian hands her the cup of water and sits on her other side, bookending her. He motions for me to join the three of them. As if this could be any more uncomfortable, the entire house reeks of their sex. I acquiesce, trying to keep the peace and sit cross-legged on the floor facing them, looking anywhere but at her.

"Everything good with the delivery?" asks Rhys. "Was Sheldon able to interrogate the vampire and figure anything out?"

It's all I can do not to laugh, though the sound wouldn't carry an ounce of mirth. Another fail. Is Mercury in retrograde? "I was able to get her to the station but when I left her in the car to grab a uniform, she broke the cuffs." And as if that weren't bad enough, I want to scream, *And then my night plummeted to the depths of hell when I walked in to find the two of you having sex in the living room with the woman I have feelings for. Without me.* Even though

I've never been involved in a threesome, that one was looking mighty good. Heat rises to my face and I scrub it with my hand, hoping no one notices.

Rhys shakes his head. "Vampire cuffs are unbreakable. How is that possible?"

I shrug. It's either that or give in and start screaming. "No idea. But by the time I got back to the car with two unis in tow, she'd kicked open the door and bolted."

"You lost her?" Caspian stage-whispers.

Rhys jumps up. "Let's go talk to Nolan."

The four of us head over to the Cliff, where Nolan is staying for the night.

The vampire is sitting at the kitchen table, awake and alert, as though he's been waiting for us.

"Nolan?" Rhys says. His brother drags his head up and looks at us. The movement is slow and disjointed, like his head is detached from the rest of his stone-still body.

It's apparent that something is wrong. His eyes are bloodshot. His mouth is crusted over with dried blood and saliva. And his neck is bare.

Rhys takes a step toward his brother but stops when I clamp onto his arm. "Where's your amulet?"

Nolan's mouth opens and closes several times, expelling foul-smelling air, before he says wheezes, "Master takes your girl for his bride."

When he lunges for Iphigenia, her screams fill the tiny house.

Grab the next book in the series, Radiant Light, here!

Want a FREE Novella? Fire and Fangs is a sexy, enemies to lovers, multiple partner paranormal with sword-crossing.

Looking for more electrifying reads that will leave you spellbound? Look no further than one (or all) of Chloe Adler's five sizzling paranormal romance series, totaling seventeen delectable books!

Another slow burn multiple partner saga promising a hint of darkness:

Chronicles of Tara starting with Synergist, a fantasy reverse harem with fae. Tara follows Amaya, an unlikely heroine and her five enigmatic heroes.

Fast Burn Darker Multiple Partner Books:

Destiny Chronicles beginning with Descent stars Sydney, a defiant sex worker and her five provocative heroes.

Danger after Dark beginning with Paris (but these can easily be read out of order). Each novella follows a different heroine traveling through Europe and their three dangerous heroes.

⟶ ✧ ❃ ✧ ⟵

Fast Burn Paranormal Romances:
Shadow Sisters begins with Overtaken. Each of these novels follows a different heroine but they are all tied together in a delicious love knot of desire and devotion.

⟶ ✧ ❃ ✧ ⟵

Newsletter: If you're not subscribed to Chloe's newsletter yet, please do join The Edge and receive updates on new releases, Chloe's life in Europe, exclusive author musings, advanced book excerpts and cover reveals.

⟶ ✧ ❃ ✧ ⟵

Follow Chloe on your favorite social media platform or drop her a line, she would love to hear from you!

- Instagram
- TikTok
- Facebook
- Bookbub
- Amazon
- Goodreads
- Email

Thank you for being more than just readers but also advocates for my work, spreading the word and sharing the magic with others.

~ Chloe

ALSO BY CHLOE ADLER

Grab Book 2 in Tales from the Edge - to continue Iphi's journey! Find out what happens next to Thorn, to Nolan and to the rest of Iphi's men.

～ ❖ ❁ ❖ ～

Want a FREE Novella? Subscribe to Chloe's newsletter!

Fire and Fangs is a sexy, enemies to lovers, multiple partner paranormal with sword-crossing. Subscribe to my newsletter to grab it! https://BookHip.com/QFGLCWZ

～ ❖ ❁ ❖ ～

Looking for more electrifying reads that will leave you spellbound? Look no further than one (or all) of Chloe Adler's sizzling paranormal romance series, totaling seventeen delectable books! If you want more of the Holt family and friends, move to book 1 in the Shadow Sisters series: Sadie's story in Mortal Desire.

～ ❖ ❁ ❖ ～

Fast Burn Paranormal Romances:

All your favorite side characters from Tales from the Edge

get their happily ever afters in *Shadow Sisters* beginning with Mortal Desire. Sadie Holt + Ryder. Chrysothemis Holt + Carter. Jared + Alec. And Burgundy + (you'll just have to read it to find out)…

A slow burn multiple partner saga promising a hint of darkness:

Chronicles of Tara starting with Synergist, a fantasy reverse harem with fae. Tara tells the story of Amaya, an unlikely heroine and her five enigmatic heroes.

Fast Burn Darker Multiple Partner Books:

Destiny Chronicles beginning with Descent stars Sydney, a defiant sex worker and her five provocative heroes.

Danger after Dark beginning with Paris (but these can easily be read out of order). Each novella follows a different heroine traveling through Europe and their three dangerous heroes.

Follow Chloe on your favorite social media platform or drop her a line, she would love to hear from you!

- Instagram - @chloeadlerauthor
- TikTok - @chloeadlerauthor
- Facebook - facebook.com/groups/523600161317601
- Bookbub - bookbub.com/profile/chloe-adler
- Amazon - www.amazon.com/stores/Chloe-Adler/author/B06ZZ838HR
- Goodreads - goodreads.com/author/show/16722267.Chloe_Adler
- Pinterest: pinterest.com/ChloeAdlerAuthor/

I'm grateful to you for embracing my characters and their stories. Thank you for reading.

~ Chloe

Printed in Great Britain
by Amazon